Box Office Butcher

Smash Hit

By
R.W.K. Clark

Edition 1
United States Copyright Office
#TX 8-372-495 February 2017

Library of Congress Control Number: 2017907163

International Standard Book Numbers
ISBN-13: 978-0997876758 (Paperback)
ISBN-13: 978-1948312165 (Paperback)
ISBN-13: 978-1948312158 (Hardback)
ASIN: B06XCXF1JH (Kindle)

/180320

ACKNOWLEDGMENTS

I dedicate this novel to my wonderful readers and for all the amazing people I've met and those I haven't. To my family and loved ones, all your support will not be forgotten.

Thank you

PROLOGUE

The woman's mouth was gaping wide as if she were screaming in unimaginable pain, but no sound could be heard except for a guttural gurgling.

Her eyes were clamped shut hard, and she could hear the jumble of voices of the doctors and nurses who were trying desperately to guide her productively through the pain, but their words meant nothing to her right at that moment. The agony and pain came in waves that rendered her practically blind and deaf in their throes. It seemed that all she could do, all her mind would allow, was to continue to scream the soundless scream which struggled to emerge from her wide-open mouth.

"Ruth, honey, try to breathe," someone was saying.

The voice was familiar, and deep in her subconscious she knew it was her physician's nurse, Dorothy Scott. Dorothy had proven herself to be more than just the assistant to Ruth's doctor; she had proven herself to be a friend of the most sincere kind. But even Dorothy was unable to get through to Ruth in the state she was in. The fact was Dorothy was little more than a listening ear before this day; even her loyal and sincere friendship had done nothing to sway her friend from the bitterness and hatred she held deep inside of her heart. That same bitterness and hatred would prove to be the death of their relationship; Dorothy just wouldn't be able to handle it in the end.

It was a bitterness and hatred she was harboring toward the child she was laboring to deliver at that very moment.

"Ruth, listen to my voice." This was Dr. Davis' voice now. "The child is crowning, and it is going to be time to push. Here it comes… now bear down!"

He didn't have to tell her twice. For the first time in forever her mouth closed and her eyes scrunched. Her breathing stopped as she pushed, and she pushed with all the strength she had. All she wanted was for the horror and torment of bearing the forsaken child to be over. Wasn't it enough that she had to have it at all?

"Good girl," he said. "Get ready to do it again, honey. Catch your breath, and when you're ready, push!"

She obeyed, because her body made her. Dr. Davis' words meant nothing at all. When the urge passed she began to gasp for breath once again. The medical staff repeated 'good job' and 'good girl' all around. Ruth despised what she considered to be their condescending attitudes.

"One more time, Ruth, and the baby will be here," Dr. Davis said. "One, two, three, push!"

She complied, and it turned out to be the shortest, fastest push out of all of them. She bore down for a few seconds, and suddenly the body that had been living and moving inside of her shot out from between her legs with such force that she thought it might have taken her insides with it. Ruth wouldn't have been surprised if it did; it was a monster, after all.

Suddenly, loud, healthy screams filled the air, and the medical staff oohed, aahed, and cheered. Ruth, overcome with sudden exhaustion, kept her eyes closed and focused on breathing. The sound of the child screaming was shut off to her; she had no interest in its wails.

"It's a boy, Ruth!" Dorothy said, her tears touching her voice. "And he is perfect— beautiful!"

Ruth Cannon kept her eyes closed while nurses ran around to tend to the tiny new life. She didn't want anyone to think she was interested in anything that took place there. She wanted to wake up and have it all, the entire last ten months, be a horrible dream. But even she knew that was too much to ask for. It was what it was, so they should just let her stay in her own little world.

But Dorothy would not let her. "Here he is, Ruth. Time to hold him; time to see if he'll nurse."

Ruth's eyes flew open and focused on her friend, who was standing beside her holding the swaddled infant. Dorothy was smiling and a single tear ran down her left cheek. Ruth shook her head violently, anger blazing in her eyes.

"But Ruth, now is the time to bond," the woman continued. "You decided to keep him; this time is essential to both of you."

Ruth closed her eyes once again, and this time she shook her head with vigorous force. Everyone in the room went silent with shock, but she didn't care. None of them understood anyway. Not one of them had any true comprehension of what she was going through or how she felt, so as far as she was concerned they could all take their sideways glances and put them where the sun don't shine.

Dorothy Scott looked around at everybody, then said, "I'll just take him to the nursery and get him cleaned up right. You take some time, okay? I'll be back in a while."

Ruth didn't respond; she simply kept her eyes closed and her head turned away.

When Dorothy left the room the others went to work on Ruth, stitching her up and dealing with the placenta. They worked in silence, unsure of how to act toward a woman who just refused, and adamantly at that, to hold her own newborn son. One by one, as they completed their tasks, they left the room to move on to other things. At last, the only one left was Dr. Davis. He pulled up a metal stool and sat next to Ruth.

"I understand the circumstances of this birth, Ruth. After all, I have been with you through the entire pregnancy," he began. "And we tried to deal with this in a number of ways. You knew your options: adoption or to keep the child. You were determined to keep the child. Now it is time for you to get over the circumstances under which he arrived. Time to be a mother. Unless you have decided to put him up for adoption, of course."

Ruth shook her head. She could feel tears of frustration welling up behind her eyes. She would keep the boy, but she had her own reasons.

"Good," he continued as he patted her shoulder. "Now, get it in your mind that you are needed by the boy and get with the program. Have you decided on a name?"

Ruth nodded, and the doctor pulled a pad out of the jacket he had put back on after he cleaned up. He handed the item to her, along with a pen. Ruth hadn't been able to speak since becoming pregnant, and she could communicate only through writing.

"Donovan James," she wrote.

She handed the items back to him, then turned away. She didn't want to deal with him, or this reality, any sooner than she had to. It seemed to her that time had given her a few extra moments to pull herself together before she had to face her decision to keep the little demon.

"That's a good, strong name, Ruth." Dr. Davis stood and looked down at his grieving patient. He hoped that she would pull out of it, that she would come around to her responsibility, but his knit brow said he doubted it. Ruth Cannon suffered from some serious post-traumatic stress.

"I'll be in to check on you once before I leave," he said, "then I'll see you tomorrow. Try to rest, Ruth; you'll need it."

With that he was gone. She turned her head and stared at the closed door he had walked through and sneered. No one understood, and they never would. Didn't they know she hadn't chosen to keep the baby out of love or desire? No! This had nothing to do with either of those.

This was about indirect revenge, and she was sure it would make her feel better about everything in the end.

About fifteen minutes passed when Dorothy returned to the room. She was carrying the infant in her arms. He was wrapped in a clean blue blanket and sported a tiny blue stocking cap on his head. He was rooting around, his eyes tightly closed, trying to find a breast he could suckle. As Dorothy stood next to the bed she held the child's head up in the crook of her elbow so Ruth could see him.

"Isn't he just beautiful?" she asked.

Ruth smirked and closed her eyes to keep the tears from coming. After a moment she opened them and gave Dorothy a single nod, indicating she was ready to try to hold and feed him. Dorothy understood right away, and she smiled with relief.

"Breastfeeding can be difficult for some," the nurse continued. "I will help you so you can adjust as quickly as possible."

Once she made sure that Ruth was holding him properly, she helped guide the boy's mouth to Ruth's nipple. He was starving, and he began to suckle furiously. The initial pain caused Ruth to cry out and wince, but she simply ground her teeth together and determined to get over it.

After a short while Dorothy said, "I'm going to go start the birth record paperwork. Will you be okay for a bit, Ruthie?"

Ruth nodded, her eyes still closed. As soon as she heard the door to her room close she opened her eyes and looked down at the nursing infant in her arms. Donovan, she thought to herself with disgust. It was a name she had always hated, so it was perfect for a child she loathed just as much.

You are the only justice I am going to have, she thought to herself as she watched him with a sneer. You will never know my love, because I promise I will never give it to you.

Once more she closed her eyes and laid her head back. The slurping sounds the kid made turned her stomach. This nursing thing was going to be the worst part, but it was essential to keep him alive.

He had to be alive if she was going to pay him back for all the pain he had, and was going to, cause her.

R.W.K. Clark

CHAPTER 1

"I can't wait until Friday. I mean, it's supposed to be the very best movie ever!"

The Los Angeles sun shined brightly down on the two girls as they made their way up the walk toward Gatewood High School. It loomed massively before them, and students milled around both the building and the girls as they strolled for the building and chatted. The sound of laughter and joking filled the fall air, and the entirety of the morning reeked of carefree contentment.

"My mom and dad told me last night that I can't go." Jennifer Schmidt's voice was heavy with disappointment. "You know how they are: no chaperone, you don't go alone. Knowing my luck I won't even be able to get married until I'm in my forties."

Her best friend, Lauren Connors, stopped dead in her tracks and turned to her. "What do you mean you can't go? Why didn't you tell me this on the phone last night?"

"I didn't find out until we hung up," the girl replied. "The worst part is that this is the one movie I have actually been waiting for. Ever since I found out that the new Miles March movie was coming out I have been planning for it. Ugh, I feel sick over it. But what can I do? There is no way my parents are going to allow me to attend something in the dark with boys around. You know this, Lauren."

Lauren smiled at her slyly. "Sneak out. I don't know. Maybe tell them you're babysitting for someone and go anyway."

"It'll never work," Jennifer said. "They call and check on me every time I babysit, and they call on the house phone where I am. I can't even lie because they won't call my cell."

Lauren shook her head with frustration. "Listen, your parents are always going out on the weekend. Maybe they will this Friday too."

They started walking again once they took notice that the crowd of kids was starting to dwindle. "They are going out! They have some kind of benefit banquet for some stupid charity my mom is into, the 'Child Victims Rights Fund', some abused children's education thing. But if I were to get caught that would mean all hope of getting a car for my sixteenth birthday would be shot. They wouldn't just threaten like your parents; they'd make me wait until next year for sure."

The girls picked up their pace, and Lauren said, "Look, today is only Monday. All you have to do is definitely not mention the movie between now and then. They're so busy it will slip their minds that you wanted to go, if it hasn't already. I mean, when was the last time you mentioned the movie to them at all? Then you come with me and Chad, and the three of us get the crap scared out of us together. We'll even go to the first showing; you'll be home by nine."

"It's gonna sell out fast, Lauren," Jennifer replied as they climbed the main steps and rushed through the doors.

"We'll just get our tickets online, like today, while we're at school."

This frustrated Jennifer even more. "How? With what? My parents don't let me have endless access to the family credit card like yours do. It won't work."

"Then I'll buy yours for you," Lauren said lightly. "You can do my algebra homework to pay me back."

Jennifer couldn't help but smile. She wasn't the kind to openly disobey her parents, but sometimes they were just a pain in the keister. After all, it was only a movie, and probably every kid her age in school was going to be seeing it. Her parents wouldn't be home until eleven or twelve on Friday, and she knew she could get away with it, but thinking about it made her nervous. The very thought of both seeing the new Miles March film and sneaking out to do it brought a double dose of butterflies to her stomach, and she liked it.

"Fine," she conceded. "You buy, I pay back somehow, but I'm not sure about doing your math, Lauren. You need to learn this too, you know."

Lauren gave her a slap on the shoulder as they stopped in front of Jennifer's English classroom. "You got it, sister. See you in study hall."

Jennifer pushed all thoughts of the movie from her mind as best she could for the rest of the day. It proved difficult; after all, it seemed that every other student at Gatewood talked about the movie all day long. She didn't let herself think about it until she got home that afternoon.

She walked into her front door to find a house so still and quiet one might have thought it was abandoned; nothing new to Jennifer. With a doctor for a father and an attorney mother, finding anyone at home after school was rare indeed. She had long since stopped caring.

"Hey, everybody, I'm home," she stated blandly.

She didn't shout the phrase, rather, she said it sarcastically and slightly under her breath. Jennifer put her bag on the stairs to take to her room and headed for the kitchen for a snack. At least there was always more than enough food in the refrigerator. It wasn't that her parents were poor parents; they provided richly for their only daughter, and they taught her responsibility and right from wrong. They were just never around; their attention was spread far too thin.

She glanced through the fridge and freezer before settling on a box of pizza rolls. As she put them on a plate and into the microwave she thought about how her father hated such treats, but he was gone so often that he had no say in what kind of food was purchased. Her mother was simply careful on nights they all three ate together, making sure to prepare and serve healthy meals, and it kept her out of the doghouse with Pops. Jennifer smiled slightly at her own thoughts as she set the timer on the microwave with anticipation and poured a glass of milk.

"Sorry, Pops, but I'm not too sorry."

Finding a music video on the small flat screen hanging on the kitchen wall made the snacks taste even better, and soon she was heading up to her room to hit the books. But by the time she had all of her homework done she was still alone in the house, and she was more than ready to hit the sack. She showered, then got comfortable in her bed before fetching her cell and speed dialing Lauren.

"Hey, girl! What's up?" Lauren's greeting was always the same.

"I'm gonna crash," she replied. "Thought I'd say goodnight. Did you work on that history report any?"

"Of course not! And g'nite, then," Lauren said. "Better rest up. I have a ticket for you for Friday. Pray the week flies by, okay?"

Jennifer felt a surge of joy. She was going to get out of the house for a change, and she couldn't wait, not to mention the fact that her outing consisted of seeing the new Miles March movie. "Thank you, girl! I'll be more than ready, and I will pay you back ASAP."

She hung up and pulled a celebrity magazine out from her nightstand drawer. The cover featured a photo of Miles March, producer and director extraordinaire. He was so handsome, with dark hair and light blue eyes that were full of confidence. Jennifer wondered if he was married; nothing she had ever read about him really gave the answer. All she knew was that he had put out some of the best scary movies ever, and his new one, *Smash Hit*, was supposed to be the best yet.

She was sure it would be like most, but according to all articles both the effects and the plot were haunting and very realistic. Critics said it was simply 'not your run-of-the-mill horror tale'. Jennifer, being the March fan she was, was more than willing to be scared to her own death. What a way to go, huh?

She set her alarm and snuggled in, a slight smile on her face as she considered the horrors that were waiting for her and her friends on Friday night.

CHAPTER 2

The packed crowd of teenagers and adults milling out of the Savoy Multiplex building was nothing short of chaotic. Teens jumped all over each other, feigning murder by stabbing or slashing. Girls screamed as boys snuck from corners and grabbed them. It was nearly impossible to get through the main doors to the parking lot, but after a long struggle Jennifer, Lauren, and Lauren's boyfriend Chad finally stepped into the cool air of the night. It was like escaping prison.

The excitement in the air was like electricity for all leaving the movie. As the three started walking away from the theater they stopped and turned to see all the other kids. The parking lot was as loud and obnoxious as the lobby inside had been, but it was far easier to enjoy the comedic scenery in a spacious place. The kids found themselves laughing and joking with all who walked near them, until they split off to head in their own direction.

The three of them had met at Delphi Park and then walked to the movie earlier that evening. Neither of the girls had their licenses yet, and Chad, who was eighteen, had had his car taken away by his father, some big hot-shot executive. It seemed that Chad had pulled in nothing higher than a 'D' on the last two report cards, and he had even tried to cover up the first report, and pretty much got away with it, too. At least, he did until the school called his father about the second one. Then the jig was up.

"What did you think? Was that the craziest, or what?" Chad's eyes were alight with the post-horror film excitement, just like everyone else's. "What was your favorite part, Lauren?"

The girl shivered. "I don't know if I had a favorite part. It's pretty spooky to go to a movie where kids are getting killed off after a movie, and then get up and leave the theater. I'll have to think about it. Did you have a favorite part, Jen?"

"I wouldn't say 'favorite', but there was a part that spooked me the worst," she replied as she glanced around them.

Lauren and Chad waited for her to tell them, then lost their patience. "What was it?"

"It was the part where the girl and her friend, in the beginning, left the theater and were walking home, just like we are right now," she said. "I guess the way the guy approached them, and they were so willing to talk to him, thinking they could trust him. That creeped me out the worst, yeah. And now here we are, walking home." She smiled, but she was shivering from the memory.

The trio continued to recall scenes and banter playfully back and forth for several blocks, then Chad said, "Here's my turn. Are you two gonna be okay? You don't expect the Box Office Butcher to get you, do ya?"

His reference to the movie made both the girls smile. Lauren and Chad embraced to say goodbye, so Jennifer began to slowly walk from them. Best to give them privacy, even if they were on a dark, quiet street. The night was still, and the air was the perfect temperature. She closed her eyes and inhaled deeply; the scents around her made her smile.

Suddenly a hand came clasping down hard on her shoulder. Jennifer jumped and screamed, spinning around to see Lauren nearly in silent hysterics. She wanted to slap her friend.

"Oh, my, Lauren! What the heck?" Her hand was on her heart, and the beating of it was like a drum beating like mad in her chest. "That's not right! It's just not right!"

Lauren got herself under control. "Sorry. You're right. I would have been triple pissed if you did it to me. Let's go, girl."

The girl grabbed Jennifer by the hand and they began to walk once again. "I think I should sneak away and marry Chad, don't you?"

"Um, you're fifteen," Jen retorted, a bit of stupid shock to her voice. "He won't even graduate at the rate he's going. Just wait. I mean, if it's meant to be, it's meant to be."

"Hey!"

A loud shout from behind them startled both of them this time. They turned simultaneously to see who it was. Lauren immediately gave a broad smile.

"He wants another kiss, see? Be right back."

The girl immediately began to jog toward her beau eagerly, but Jennifer stayed behind, blushing a bit. She was a tad bit jealous; having a boyfriend would be nice. But she had other plans for now, like preparing for her future. Sometimes she wished Lauren would think a bit responsibly.

Lauren approached Chad, and Jennifer could hear her giggle, and then the girl said something else, but Jen couldn't make it out. Suddenly, just as she reached him, Jennifer realized something wasn't right. It happened so quickly she almost couldn't put a finger on it. Then it hit her: he seemed to be wearing Chad's school jacket, but as Lauren neared she knew the guy was way too tall, in comparison to Lauren, to be Chad.

The man drew up with his arm and then swooped it downward violently, in what appeared to be a punch. Lauren uttered a guttural scream, and he repeated the action, but when he pulled back Jennifer saw a stream of blood fly through the air, even reaching beneath the nearby street light. Then again, and again, and again, until Lauren was on the ground and he was just pummeling her.

Jennifer was frozen in place. She couldn't scream, but in her mind she was bellowing with all she had.

Suddenly it occurred to her that she was standing there, and he seemed to be wrapping things up.

She took off from her place like a shot. The man's head shot up just in time to see her round a corner and disappear from sight, and he jumped up to take after her. A large knife with a pair of prongs at the tip was clutched in his right hand, and he wore a mask over the bottom part of his face, though his hair was natural and free. He was smiling as he ran, because the chase was his favorite part.

But when he turned the corner Jennifer was nowhere to be found. The street was completely dead and silent, and there was no way for him to track her down. He turned and pulled his mask off. As he headed to a grouping of bushes near the girl's body he wrapped his knife in the mask and tucked it into an inside pocket on his coat. Soon he was crouching in the shrubbery, and he had a perfect view of her blood-soaked body. She was dead, all right.

One down, six to go.

R.W.K. Clark

CHAPTER 3

Little did the girl know her parents were already home, had discovered her absence, and were thankfully waiting to confront her. Regardless, her punishment was the furthest thing from any of their minds after she returned crying hysterically and trying to tell them what had happened to Lauren.

The driveway at Jennifer Schmidt's house sported two police cruisers parked out front, their lights still flashing. There had been three police cars, but one of them left to meet an ambulance at the location where Jennifer told them Lauren had been killed. She had already related the entire story to both her parents and then again to police. Now, she sat in a semi-trance, exhausted, remembering the violent attack on her friend. The movie they had left prior to Lauren's murder was the furthest thing from her mind.

A young officer with blond hair and a police radio in his hand entered through the front door after rapping briefly.

"Ma'am, sir, I'm Officer Carson," he said to her parents, then to a suited detective. "Detective Harmes, can I speak to you over here, please?"

The detective who had been taking Jennifer's statement rose and let them know he would be right back, but the girl had no awareness of anything being said around her. All she could see in her mind was her friend being hacked to death, and she was in a serious state of shock. Even her mother's murmuring in her ear did nothing to pull her into reality.

The detective returned and took his seat. "Jennifer," he began. "Listen, honey, I know how difficult this is for you, and I can't imagine your pain. But I need you to stay with us right now. We need you if we are going to catch the guy who did this to your friend Lauren."

After a moment she looked at him, her eyes searching his face. She heard what he said, and something inside of her was able to grasp it correctly. He was right; her best friend in the world had been murdered, but she was safe. She needed to be tough.

"Okay," she said in nothing more than a whisper. "But I've told you everything; what more can I do?"

His face gave off as much compassion as he could muster, and he spoke in the softest, gentlest voice he had. "I need you to go over everything again. At first I was going to say that Chad Bryant, the boyfriend, was our prime suspect. Unfortunately, Chad's body was found in an alley just a block away from his house. I need you to go over everything from the beginning."

Jennifer's eyes grew wide and filled with tears yet again. Her face had changed as well, as though she had just come to some type of realization. She shook her head and let the tears fall freely.

"It's just like the movie! Don't you see, it's just like the movie!"

"The movie you were at before the incident?" Detective Harmes asked.

She nodded rapidly. "Yes! In the first murder there were two girls walking alone in the scene, but they had been with the first victim's boyfriend! The three of them separated at the theater, and she got killed by someone who looked familiar and called her back! Just like Lauren. After that, the boyfriend was found dead, too! Oh, no, I'm going to be sick!"

Jennifer jumped up from her chair and disappeared from the room. Harmes began to rub his forehead as though he could feel a headache coming on. "Dr. and Mrs. Schmidt, I really need her to go over things again. This new case with the young man, well, threw me. Threw all of us here, as a matter of fact. Now your daughter brings up a scene in the movie that reminds her of the murders. I'm starting to think some sick high-schooler decided to act out some fantasy and gave double homicide a try."

"Listen, Detective," Ralph Schmidt said in an icy voice, "I think it's time for me to give her a sedative and put her to bed. She has suffered a terrifying trauma. As her father, I'm concerned for her state of mind. As a doctor, her health. I must insist we put the rest of this interview off until tomorrow."

"I understand," Harmes replied as he rose to his feet once again. "Can you bring her to the station in the morning, let's say around ten?" He flipped a business card out of his suit jacket and handed it to the man. "I will be there bright and early, if I even go home tonight. I probably won't see a day off until we catch this guy."

"Sure. Ten o'clock," Ralph Schmidt replied with a resigned nod. The man looked tired to Harmes. "Thanks for understanding."

Hands were shaken all around, and then Mr. Schmidt went after his daughter to take care of her. Her mother saw everyone out and closed up the house. As Harmes stood out by his car he saw the lights on the lower level of the house being turned off one by one.

There was a maniac running around somewhere out there, and obviously Mrs. Schmidt didn't want him anywhere near her family.

CHAPTER 4

The only light in the room was the reflective flickering of a large flat-screen television set. It was mounted above a fireplace, but there was no fire. Just the movie playing, the sound at a minimum, the bluish light flickering off of everything in the dark space around it.

The man sat in a reclining red leather chair, but it was in the upright position. His arms were placed casually and comfortably on the armrests, as if he were meditating or napping. But while his head was resting back his eyes were wide open, and they were focused on the bloody images splashing across the screen. The fingers on his right hand twitched in time with the stabbing and screaming on the set on the wall.

"Finish her," he hissed with a sneer.

Suddenly, the killer in the movie pulled the girl's head back by her long, lush hair. She let out begging sobs, but to no avail. Suddenly, with a single swing of his arm and slash of his knife the girl was finished. He found the entire scene was more than exhilarating, no matter how many times he had viewed it. The scene gave the man great… release.

Now, the man in the chair let out a long, ragged breath. He had been in ecstasy when he killed the girl earlier that night. The boy's murder happened out of both planning and necessity, and it had been quick and easy. After all, he needed the kid's high school jacket if he was going to get anywhere near his true target, and his ploy had worked like a charm. It was also very important that he stay as faithful to the script as was humanly possible.

He thought he had done a wonderful job.

Watching the movie which the two murders had been based on again wasn't nearly as good, though the scene he had copied had made him excited when he viewed it.

He had gone to the movie and sat way up in the balcony. It was important to pick the right ones, so observation was key. In the meantime he had taken video of the entire movie on his cell phone. That way he had it handy, not that he needed it. Perhaps he simply enjoyed its company.

His first victims had been easy enough to select, and with the size of the crowd, tailing them on foot had been like taking candy from a baby. It honestly had taken little to no effort to choose, and he chose well. Now he relished the memory of the First Act.

He always knew just what to do; after all, he was Miles March's biggest fan, bigger than any of them. No one knew better than he what Miles March was capable of creating. But he did, and he would make sure the rest of the world learned it too.

He smiled as he watched the same scene yet again. He would be rewinding several times before the night was over. After all, he had to be good and ready for his next date.

Another masterpiece in the making.

∞

"I can't tell you how much we appreciate you coming down this morning, Jennifer." Detective Harmes placed a can of diet soda on the table in front of her. "You look like you feel better. How are you doing?"

Jennifer shrugged her shoulders. "As good as could be expected, I guess," she replied. "You want me to tell you what happened again, right?"

Ralph Schmidt interjected. "My daughter may still be a little woozy from the sedative I administered last night, so please be patient with her."

Harmes nodded at the man and turned to Jennifer. "Again, I'm sorry to put you through this. Ready?" The girl gestured that she was, so he pressed the button on a small, handheld recorder. "This is Detective Kevin Harmes with the Los Angeles Police Department, Homicide Division. This is the statement of Jennifer Schmidt regarding the murders of Lauren Connors and Chad Bryant. The date is October 14, 2016, and the time is 1005 hours. Go ahead, Jennifer."

The girl began to speak, telling her perspective on the events which had taken place the night before. She started with her and her two friends leaving the movie, and told Harmes how the three of them had walked a specific amount of distance before Chad parted ways with them. Jennifer related exactly what street he turned down to go home, and she also told the detective, with tears in her eyes, how Lauren had frightened her for fun, and the way her best friend had laughed about it. Finally, the girl began to tell, in detail, what happened next.

"When Lauren was done teasing with me, we took each other by the hand and began to walk again. The street was dark, but the street lights were on. I didn't feel threatened; we were both in a good mood. She was even talking about running away to marry Chad."

Jennifer paused and snatched a tissue from a box on the table, which she used to blow her nose. "Then, while we were walking, someone yelled, 'hey!'."

"Was it a man's voice, Jennifer?" Detective Harmes asked gently.

The girl's head bobbed up and down. Tears were forming in her cloudy eyes, and one trickled down her already-wet cheek. "Yeah. It was a man's voice. It was deep, I guess. Deeper than Chad's. I don't know why I didn't think of it then. We turned to see who it was, and it looked like Chad, even to me. He had his school jacket on and everything. He was just standing there, right at the intersection where Chad had actually turned.

He was wearing a Gatewood High jacket, and we both thought it was Chad!"

Tears were pouring out quickly now, so Harmes paused and plucked a couple more tissues free and handed them to the distraught young high-schooler. There were always so many victims when a life was taken; Lauren and Chad had been two of them. All of the people who knew them would be forever changed, and it made him sick.

After another nose-blow Jennifer continued. "Lauren thought that Chad wanted another goodbye kiss." Jennifer smiled at the memory. "She took off toward him. I stayed where I was; nobody likes to be the third wheel. I remember feeling a little jealous. You know, because they were so in love. Now I feel guilty for thinking that way. I have the rest of my life to find my love; poor Lauren will never even go to prom!"

She broke out in yet another burst of tears. Harmes always appreciated the moments when the crying came. It gave him time to think ahead, and it gave the grieved time to process. He was patient every time.

"Exactly when did you know something wasn't right, Jennifer?" Harmes was able to ask at last.

The teenager's face immediately scrunched up yet again as she recalled the incident. "It seems to me that something inside of me knew he wasn't right from the start. He was under the street light, but his face was all shadows. But what got my attention was when Lauren got... got up closer to him. Something in my mind was thinking that Chad had gotten taller. Then I realized that the person was a lot taller compared to Lauren than Chad was. The guy was just way too tall."

Jennifer paused for a moment before letting her words come out in a rush of emotion all at once. "I wish I hadn't let Lauren go back. I should have grabbed her arm and made her go home. I should have dragged her if I had to, but I didn't. I should have dragged her kicking and screaming down the street!"

But Harmes knew there was no way to change the facts: she hadn't, and what was done was done. He nodded with sympathy and remained still as the girl cried in the interview room for the last time. He thought she would want to stop, and he was surprised when she abruptly stopped crying and continued.

Jennifer took a sharp, deep breath. "All of a sudden the man lifted his arm in the air and swung his fist down at her. I thought he punched her; that was how it looked to me. But when he pulled his fist back blood just went flying!" She stopped again, this time with tears falling down her face like spigots had been turned on behind her eyes, but she didn't let out a single sob. She just stared down at her hands in her lap, her eyes leaking profusely.

"Can we take a break?" Celia Schmidt was getting alarmed. "Maybe she just needs to take a little breather." The woman had begun gently massaging her daughter's shoulders.

"I'm fine." Jennifer held up her hand and got her breathing under control. "It was when I saw all that blood that I knew he was stabbing her, and he did it over and over and over again. I couldn't move; I should have, but I just couldn't. It was like I froze up, and all I could do was watch what was happening. Now it seems like it all happened in slow motion, like it wasn't even real at all. I'm sorry, Lauren; I'm just so sorry."

Detective Harmes clicked the recorder off. "Jennifer. Take your time; take a break like your mom said, if you want."

The stubborn girl shook her head and turned to her mother. "You just have to understand that I am going to cry. But no matter what, I have to do this; I'm the only one who can."

She reached forward and plucked another tissue from a box on the table, wiped her eyes, blew her nose, and kept going.

"I was frozen, but I realized it all of a sudden. I took off from there so fast, and I knew he saw me because I could feel his eyes. Then, as I ran, I could hear his steps around the corner. He had started to come after me, but I was long gone. I hid behind Mr. Martenson's car port, and I watched the guy come around the corner. He stopped and looked around for a second, then ran back in the direction we came from. I went home as fast as I could. That's it, Detective Harmes. That's all that I saw."

The room became still once again, and Harmes turned off the recorder for good. He looked at her for a moment. "Off the record for now, kid, what were you saying about it being just like in the movie?" He wanted to clarify first; if he let her tell him on the recorder it would sound like nothing but rantings, and it would negate the rest of the statement. But he wanted to know, because everything was important at this stage in the game.

"Like I said, it was just like in the movie." Now her eyes brightened a bit, but not out of happiness. She had been thinking about the similarities all morning, and she was glad to have someone listen. "When I was walking with Lauren and Chad, he had asked us what our favorite parts were. I told him about the first murder scene. I was telling them about this scene because I thought it was the scariest."

"What was scary about it?" Harmes asked.

Jennifer gave an almost embarrassed shrug. "In the movie two friends are walking home, and some guy hollers at them from, like, a block away. The girls think they know him, and one of them heads back to him, but he's the killer. Just like what happened to Lauren. Exactly the same."

Kevin Harmes didn't respond. He was thinking about what the girl had just told him and watching her face closely. Yep, he thought. It was probably some overzealous horror fan who had done this tragic thing.

He was more than ready to track down the little menace and make him pay.

R.W.K. Clark

CHAPTER 5

The man hung up the phone and strolled over to the window. It was a beautiful sunny day, a day which made him look forward to the night, which was sure to come. He had had an appointment that evening, but he had cancelled it. There were more important things to do. The ball was rolling now; it was vital to keep it that way.

Picking up the telephone once again he made a series of short calls, then hung it up once and for all. Now it was time to focus on priorities. After all, if he wanted to prove he was the greatest, he couldn't afford to be a slacker in any department.

Next he made his way to the large oak entertainment cabinet in the corner. He opened it and, after turning on the television set inside, pressed play on the DVD player, then sat down. The second murder scene of *Smash Hit* began exactly where he wanted it to. It was time to prepare for the Second Act of his 'homework'.

A young bimbo, long blond hair and pretty blue eyes, was just getting home from the theater, from watching a horror movie with friends. She lived alone in a small bungalow at the end of a quiet street, and she was a bit frightened. The movie had managed to spook her quite a bit; even as she unlocked her front door she looked around, here and there. As soon as she had the door open she reached inside and turned on the living room light, then made the rounds and turned all the lights on in her house.

Now she was warming up a slice of cold pizza in her microwave. She turned the radio on and began to sing freely with the song that was playing, a poppy, bubblegum-type song that happened to be at the top of the charts among listeners her age. Then, in the unfocused background, the stranger appeared. His face could not be seen, and she didn't hear him due to the music. He stood and watched her in silence, a long, sharp knife in his hand being held casually at his side. He was nothing more than an outline, a blur, a shadow of what was to come.

Suddenly, the girl turned; she saw him right away. One scream and he moved with the grace and speed of a cat, charging her and delivering a single forceful blow to her head. She went flying into the small kitchen table and chairs, and she crumpled to the floor, moaning and writhing in pain. Her long blond hair was mussed, and it was covering her face. He walked over to the radio and turned it up loud. The girl did this all the time, he knew. The neighbors would think nothing of it. When he turned back around she was scrambling out of the kitchen, and he couldn't help but smile. The thrill of the chase and all. He even began to whistle to the annoying tune that was playing.

Calmly, he began to pursue her. Just like all of them, she sniveled and cried and tripped over everything in sight. He stopped and watched her make it to the front door; it was very entertaining to see her act out of fear. She fumbled with the locks, unlocking all of them, then trying to open it. Poor girl; in her hysteria she hadn't taken notice of the newly installed padlock on the door at the very top. He stood and watched, amused and entertained as she yanked and tugged and screamed for help. When she finally accepted that the door was not going to open she bolted for the hallway, and he heard her bedroom door slam shut.

With a grin and a cluck of the tongue he started for the bedroom, where she thought she had holed up enough to slow him down. When he got to the door he grasped the knob and tried to turn it, but of course she had thrown the lock. The killer didn't play around; he gave the door one powerful kick and it flew inward. The girl was on the bed, sobbing hysterically, trying to get the window up.

"That window has been painted shut for years," he told her in a calm, soothing voice. "You know that, Erika. It's senseless to fight, you know. This is your destiny."

She jumped up from the bed, stumbled for a second, then tried to run past him, but he grabbed her lush mane of hair and flung her down to the floor. She looked up at him as he lifted the knife and waved it around.

"No! Please!"

Scrambling on her hands and knees, Erika tried to crawl across the room. He let her, for a moment. Soon he was on her, and he grabbed her violently by her long hair, pulling her head back with a snap. With a single deft movement he slashed at her throat, and the blood came pouring out in great rushes. It ran over his hands, soaking his gloves. The killer's eyes glazed over from the feeling of the blood's warmth; oh, how he wished he could have bare hands when he worked!

When she had bled out he stood back and watched the girl twitch and gurgle one last time as her final breath left her body, but as soon as she stopped moving he became instantly bored. He put his knife in his coat pocket, and as calmly as you please he walked through the house and out the back door.

He was smiling, because it had been just that simple.

With the remote control the man turned off the movie. He didn't need to watch it again; he already had hundreds of times. He was ready. He even had the girl picked out, as he had for some time. This was a vital and perfect part of the big picture.

Tonight would be her night; time for the Second Act.

Detective Kevin Harmes sat in his office playing the recording of Jennifer Schmidt's statement. It was solid, just like the first time she related the murder to him in her home. Nothing had changed. The difference was her detailing a bit more about the movie scene she compared Lauren's murder to.

That bit of information had him, and it wouldn't let go. It was the movie thing; Jennifer said the murder was the same as the first murder in the movie. Kevin had always loved horror films when he was a kid, but he didn't have a lot of time as he got older to indulge. The passion had slipped away.

He thought he might make it a point to go see it. Maybe even that night. According to the news it was sweeping the box office off its feet. Well, if he had time he would have to give it a look-see. He was sure his hunch about an eager horror fan being the perp was correct; he was just morbidly curious how close the perp had gotten the real murder or murders to those acted out on the big screen.

Just that quickly, *Smash Hit* left his thoughts. Of course the murderer was some kid who had watched it the night before and decided to get a rush! The next sensible step was to start talking to high schoolers. After all, they were the ones who had attended the most. Someone, somewhere knew something.

Harmes stood up, grabbed his notebook, and put his coat on. Time to get to work and find this guy.

Unfortunately, the only way to go about doing that at this point was to pound the pavement and knock on doors.

It was going to be a long Saturday, but he planned on having a good time hunting.

CHAPTER 6

"Hey, Kelly, someone sent me tickets to see that new horror movie *Smash Hit* tonight. Do you want to go with me?"

Shannon Helms had very few friends in the Los Angeles area. As a matter of fact, if Kelly Packard weren't her friend she would have none. She had lived in the city two months, having relocated from Idaho to work for her uncle in his law firm. It was a job which would help her earn enough money to go to law school herself. It also helped that her father had rented her the cute little cottage at the end of the dead-end on Charleston Street. Otherwise, she would never be able to save.

"Who sent them to you?" Kelly asked.

Shannon's brow knit. "I'm not sure; I think someone from the office. I just got them last night, and it's Saturday, so I probably won't find out until Monday, but I'm sure it's someone from work. If it wasn't you, and you say it wasn't, then our co-workers are the only people left. So, are you game? I don't really want to go alone."

"I can't, Shannon. I'm sorry." Kelly was sincere; she had been wanting to check out the film that had been called 'the scariest movie of all time'.

Shannon rolled her eyes. "Ugh. I can't go alone. The city is so big— it's overwhelming."

"Well, the only way you are going to adjust is if you make yourself take risks," Kelly shot back. "I'm going out to dinner with Steve, and I just can't cancel. I think he is going to finally propose. Just go, Shannon. You'll enjoy it. Then, the next time we talk, I can fill you in on my date, and you can tell me all about *Smash Hit*."

Shannon offered her only friend a sigh and ran her fingers through her thick blond hair. "You're probably right. I don't know. Aw, what the hay. I'll do it."

"And give me a full report on it tomorrow, okay?"

Shannon agreed, wished her friend luck on her 'proposal' theory, and disconnected the call. She wished she had someone else to ask, but Kelly was right; time to put on her big girl panties. Maybe she would even grab a bite after the movie.

She glanced at her watch. The show time on her ticket was nine ten; that was only two hours away. What was she going to wear?

Shannon showered and went through her closet. It's not like it's a date or anything, she thought to herself. No need for fancy threads. She ended up choosing a pair of blue jeans and a lightweight sweater. After a thorough blow-dry and makeup session it was twenty minutes to nine. Time to hit the road. She grabbed her purse, locked up her house, and jumped into the sedan her parents had gotten for her when she moved to Los Angeles and her brand-new life.

As the little car sped off up the street a man stepped out from beside her house, careful to stay out of the streetlights. It was time to go inside and prepare for sweet Shannon coming home. It wouldn't take long, and he would have lots of time to go through her things and enjoy them, especially once he had the padlock installed on the front door.

He made his way to the back of the house and the window she had left cracked in the kitchen. He hummed to himself as he thought about the blond girl's blood rushing over his hands. She had been a wonderful choice, and it had been his pleasure to send her the tickets, even if she had no one to go with her. A girl with no friends does a lot of things alone.

As he cut the kitchen screen and hoisted himself into her home he thought about the first time he spotted her from his car as he was pulling out of the parking garage where he worked. She had been coming out of the fancy lawyer's practice across the street, and she was beautiful. Such a shame to put an end to such beauty, but it had to be done for the sake of the point. He chose to look at it as though he was preserving the beauty of someone like her forever, not wasting it. All of this had a very important point to it, a dire message that must be sent. Shannon and everyone else he had chosen for future 'acts' had been hand-picked by him with great care. They just didn't know it.

Inside, the man in black used his flashlight to guide him as he painstakingly installed the padlock high up on the door. Once she came home, whether she went into the bedroom, bathroom, or kitchen, he would be able to lock it without any fear of being seen. It was perfect.

When he was finished he glanced at his watch: a quarter to ten. He guessed she would be back between eleven thirty and midnight, depending on whether she stopped for food like a normal person. But it didn't matter to him.

He was, and always had been, a very patient man.

CHAPTER 7

Shannon walked out of the packed theater at five past eleven. The night air snapped her back into reality when the playful voices all around her could not. The movie had been good, probably the best horror flick she had ever seen. She was still a bit spooked.

She found her car and checked the back seat carefully: all clear. Soon, she was inside tooling down the road, thinking about what she might want to eat. Her eyes shot here and there, looking at different fast food joints, but nothing appealed to her. She decided that she would go home and heat up a can of chili instead. Fast, easy, and yummy. Anyway, she was pretty tired, and her warm bed sounded good.

Soon she was pulling her car into her drive and heading into the house. She thought she might not have chili; maybe she would fry up a single cheeseburger for herself. Shannon opened the front door and turned on the light, illuminating the living room. She locked two locks on the front door and turned on the television, making sure the volume was up high so she could hear it clearly from the kitchen. She enjoyed listening to music channels provided from her satellite television service, and her TV had awesome sound.

A pop song began to pump from the surround sound system, and Shannon immediately broke out in song. Wow, she was hungry. She had skipped snacking at the theater because the sight of blood sometimes made her sick; better for her to watch on an empty stomach.

She sang loudly as she pulled a small package of ground beef out of the refrigerator and put it to her mouth as if it were a microphone. Soon she danced it over and set it down on the counter next to the stove. Now for a pan.

Shannon turned for the pan cabinet when he filled her eyesight; she went silent immediately.

"Are you going to be a screamer?" he asked as he flashed a charming grin at her through his mask. She didn't see it, though; only his eyes were showing.

She took him in all at once, in a fraction of a second. He was tall... very tall. His hair was black and tousled, and his eyes were light blue. That was all she could see of his face; his nose, mouth, and chin were covered with a black face mask. She could see clearly by his icy eyes, however, that he was smiling.

Shannon screamed piercingly, but she knew in her thudding heart that no one would hear her; she was right on the dead-end, and on both sides of her were an empty field and a bit of woods. The nearest house was on the corner at the first turnoff up the block. She didn't need to think about her next move; she darted like a bird, shooting past him and heading to the front door of the house.

It took her no effort whatsoever to unlock the two locks, but to her dismay, and growing panic, the door would not open. Her screams continued as she pulled frantically, turning for a fraction of a second to see that her pursuer was standing, unmoving, behind her; he held a shiny knife in his right hand with two prongs on the end: a filet knife. It registered on her immediately that he was amused by her struggle with the door, and that fact made Shannon's blood run cold.

The horrified young lady darted toward the short hallway to her right. He just stood, humming along to the song filling the house. Would she go directly to the bedroom? He didn't think so, but one could hope. After all, that was where the second victim was killed in the movie.

Sure enough, she took a sharp right and disappeared from his sight. The killer gave a long sigh, as though he was beginning to get bored with the chase game, but nothing could have been further from the truth. He just knew she would go for the window in there, and he also knew it wouldn't open, thanks to a single nail he had driven through the pane to secure it tightly in place. The sigh was almost one of pity.

The door to Shannon's sleeping quarters didn't have a lock, so he took his sweet time. Rather than walk to her room he danced his way there, his moves in perfect time to the song on the television. When he rounded the corner he was pleased to see that she was on her knees on the bed, struggling with the window, just as she should have been.

"Why are you fighting all of this?" he asked.

She spun around and cried out in terror as he flashed his knife in her direction once again. Her back was up against the wall, and as she sobbed, begging for her life, she slid down into a near sitting position. It looked like she had run out of the will to fight, and this angered him a bit. He had chosen her, after all, not only for her looks, but for her guts. Not every beautiful young lady moves across the USA to start a solo life. At the sight of her crumbling he began to relax. Maybe it was for the best; it would make the killing easy, if not as thrilling as he had planned. It was vital to stay on script, though.

But she had a surprise left in her. Shannon bolted again, leaping from the bed like a cat and taking him off guard. When she ran past him he reached out to grab her hair and jerk her back, just like in *Smash Hit*, but she pulled away from him, leaving him with nothing but a handful of blond hairs and a bunch of growing rage. This wouldn't do! She was supposed to die in the bedroom!

This time when Shannon ran she went down the hall toward the back door. It has one lock, she thought. Just flip the one lock and go. But three feet from the door her foot caught a jacket, the same jacket she had reminded herself to hang up earlier, and she fell forward. In a flash the killer was on her, and with horror she realized he was laughing. It sounded evil, but even worse than that was the fact that it sounded… satisfied.

He grabbed her hair and yanked her head hard, so hard she was worried he might break her neck. But Shannon didn't have to worry about that for long. The next thing she saw was his arm swooping down and something brushing over her neck as he sliced her throat wide open. She felt no pain, but she knew what had happened, and that the life was draining out of her.

Shannon's hands went to her throat as she stared up at him with disbelief in her eyes. Blood pumped out between her fingers, soaking her sweater and pooling on the floor. He stared down at her face, his eyes dancing. Soon the girl crumpled into a near-dead heap at his feet, and he was pleased.

"You're a star!" he exclaimed.

That was the last thing Shannon Helms saw or heard in her life.

∞

Flash units popped off from digital cameras, here and there, causing Kevin Harmes to flinch nervously. He stood outside the door of the tiny bathroom in the home of one Shannon Leigh Helms, aged 23 and deceased. His stomach was flip-flopping nervously.

"Who called this in?" he asked one of the responding officers.

The man gestured with his thumb toward a pretty young woman in a professional-type skirt suit with frosted brown hair. She had tears running down her face, but her mascara was perfect. The fact that he picked up on it made him shake his head.

"What's her name?"

"Miss Kelly Packard," the cop replied, answering from his little notebook. "She works with the vic at a law firm, Bailey, Helms, and Bailey. I guess the 'Helms' is the vic's uncle. She's lived here two months, Harmes. Miss Packard is both a co-worker and Miss Helms' only local friend."

He approached the girl, who appeared to be ranting in shock to a female officer, and the woman was doing a poor job of consoling her. As she spoke to the officer her hands flailed about as if she were speaking with them rather than her mouth. It was obvious she was grief-stricken.

"Miss Packard?" Harmes held out his hand to the woman, and she responded by placing her trembling one in his and looking at him with confusion. "I'm Detective Harmes; I'm the lead on this case. I was told you are the one who called it in?" When she nodded he asked, "Can you tell me what happened?"

The young lady nodded and dabbed at her face with a sopping tissue. "I had talked to Shannon last night. I had a date, and she was going to a movie; someone had sent her a pair of tickets, but I couldn't go with her. I called her around midnight, after I had gotten home from my date. I was supposed to fill her in on whether or not my boyfriend proposed. She didn't answer, so I figured she had stopped for a drink or two and then gone to bed."

Harmes was writing furiously in his notebook. "Did she typically drink?"

Now she gave him a vigorous headshake. "No! Shannon had her head on straight; she knew what she wanted to do, and from what I could see she didn't let things deter her. All I can say is that she has a couple now and then, just like everyone, and I have never seen her drunk. I encouraged her to go out alone, so I thought maybe she had a couple to calm her nerves. Shannon was new to the area, and the city seemed to frighten her a little bit, you know?"

The girl broke out in another rash of tears, and the female officer went to get her more tissue out of a cruiser. Nose blown and eyes wiped, Kelly looked at Harmes with eyes that were finally mascara-smudged. "She didn't go out, detective. She was from Idaho. She lived here two months. I had to put heat on her to talk her into going alone, but she told me she was going, so I'm sure she did. She wouldn't lie."

"She could have changed her mind," Harmes quipped, but his mind was far from the words. His stomach had instantly begun to tremble inside when he heard the words 'new movie' and *Smash Hit*. Coincidence? He was starting to wonder.

"Someone gave her tickets, but it sounds like she didn't know anyone," Harmes asked. "Who would do that, then? Send her tickets, I mean."

"She mentioned that she thought maybe someone from work, but she got them in her mailbox Friday after she got home. She said she would find out Monday."

Harmes turned to an officer standing at the door of the house. "I need someone to put a call in to Bailey, Helms, and Bailey. Have someone there ask all around the office if anyone gave the tickets to Miss Helms." He turned back to Kelly. "Did she mention a note, or an envelope at all? Any other details about these tickets?"

Kelly shook her head slowly, her facial expression showing that she was trying to think. "No... I don't think so. She just said someone gave them to her, and she didn't know who. To be honest, I don't even think she said anything about a mailbox."

Harmes was still for a moment. "How did you get into the house, Kelly?"

"With a key."

He furrowed his brow. "Why do you have a key?"

"I don't," she replied. "Her uncle does. Stanley Helms. He gave it to me and told me to come and get her after I called and told him I couldn't get a hold of her. It was unlike her not to answer her phone. She didn't make people worry; she wasn't that kind of a girl." She blew her nose again. "I just thought she stopped for a couple after the movie and had a hangover. I didn't expect this! Oh, no, how am I going to tell Mr. Helms?"

"We'll take care of that, Kelly. Put that out of your mind." Harmes gave her a second once again, then asked: "So you came in, right? Please tell me everything; every little detail. Even if it seems silly to you."

She paused for a moment. "I figured the door was locked so I used the key. When I put it in the door I realized the door wasn't even locked, so I opened it, and I stuck my head in and yelled her name. There was no answer, so I went in and closed the door; the house was so quiet. If her car hadn't been here I would have thought she'd gone out for breakfast. I started to get a really bad feeling. First, I went into the kitchen, but she wasn't there. Next I just went for her room, and she wasn't there either. I started to look all over again, and that was when the kitchen spooked me. Raw meat on the counter, just sitting. No sound, no music, no nothing. I touched the raw meat, and it was warm.

"So I went down the back hall, toward the back door, and I was calling her name."

She stopped then, closed her eyes and put her hand over her mouth. It took Kelly three full minutes to gain her composure; Harmes just let it happen. He'd had to go through it a million times.

He turned to another officer. "I want you to check all the garbage cans, the vic's purse, desk drawers, everywhere. You are looking for an envelope, or a note, maybe. I expect any envelope you find to be empty or to have a single movie ticket inside."

The cop quickly left to inform the crime scene team, and Harmes turned back to Kelly. "I have to ask, did you disturb or touch anything in the house while you were here?"

"Just the doorknobs. I know I didn't touch anything else. Oh, yeah, I touched the meat," she replied. "And the very second I found Shannon and saw that note on her I ran out the front door and called 911 from my cell."

Harmes nodded and smiled at the girl. "Good enough," he told her as he gave her shoulder a comforting squeeze. "How about if we have Officer Gilroy here drive you home or to wherever you need to go? I will likely have to talk to you again, so I'll need your address and number. Have someone get your car for you, okay?"

She nodded, and after Harmes had jotted down her contact information the female officer led her away, an arm around her shoulders. Harmes turned his attention to the house and its gaping door and crime scene tape. Back to work.

He made his way through the house and down the short back hall of Shannon Helms' home. The crime scene team was done taking photos finally; they had been at it for two hours. The coroner was kneeling over the body filling out paperwork with gloved hands.

"Cause of death?" he asked.

She turned to him. "Single slash to the throat with an extremely sharp blade. It cut halfway through her throat. Oh, yeah, this is for you."

The woman held up a single evidence bag. Harmes stepped forward and took it from her, then held it up to the sunlight coming in through the window in the back door. It looked to be a single sheet of paper with smears of blood on it. As he looked his vision seemed to clear, and suddenly he could make out words:

"The Second Act".

Harmes' eyes grew wide and his hands shook as he looked at the coroner. "What is this?"

The woman raised her eyebrows and shook her head. "It was literally nailed to her chest. I've never seen anything like it."

Harmes released a ragged breath. "Oh, man. Tell me we don't have a serial on our hands!"

R.W.K. Clark

CHAPTER 8

First, they found a plain white envelope tucked away in Shannon's purse, which was on the kitchen table. The top had been ripped away, and it contained a single, unused ticket to the film *Smash Hit* and the stub from a second ticket. Obviously, Shannon had made it to the nine ten showing.

The words "For you... have a little fun" were scrawled in ink across the front.

Harmes had immediately bagged the envelope, ticket, and stub. Someone sent her tickets, all right, and just like Kelly said, Shannon had no way of knowing who, if that was what they arrived in.

At the crime scene, he, another detective, a uniformed officer, and a couple of guys from CSU also attempted to recreate the murder of Shannon Helms.

"So, she comes in the door," said the other detective, Joe Carter. "I assume she didn't lock it behind her."

Harmes bristled. "Why? Because he got her in her house? He could have been inside already, for all we know."

A knock came from the other side of the door, and Harmes jerked it open to see a very young beat cop on the other side. "One of the neighbors would like to speak to you, sir."

Harmes looked out to see a woman of about fifty. She was pulling a sweater tightly around her shoulders, and she looked creeped out to even be there. He took note of her eyes darting to and fro as he made his way in her direction.

"I'm Detective Harmes. How can I help you?"

"I'm Shirley Catman," she said with a shaking voice. "I live just up there on the corner. I heard what happened to that poor girl."

Harmes nodded. He was anxious to get back to his investigation. "Did you see something you want to tell me about?"

"No, no. But something I heard is what is bothering me."

Harmes raised his eyebrows and waited.

"This girl, I didn't really know her except to wave now and then," Shirley said. "But I'm a watcher since my husband died, and I try to keep an eye out for neighbors. This girl was a creature of habit. Did the same exact things every day, ever since she moved in. As a matter of fact, last night was the first time she broke her routine that I had ever seen."

"Go on."

"Well, yesterday about fifteen minutes before nine, give or take, I was at my kitchen sink, which is facing the street here," she told him. "I saw her little red car pass by, and I remember thinking, 'Good. She's getting out of the house', and I thought no more of it. I even smiled a little, thinking maybe she had met someone and had a date. She was such a pretty girl, and she seemed to really have a good head on her shoulders.

"Anyway, every evening when she comes home from work she would do the same thing: put on music from the TV. I know it was from the television by the way the lights flickered in her living room. She would turn it up loud. Nothing that would bother me, mind you, but louder than the average person. She asked me once if it bothered me; she said it was the only way she could hear it in her kitchen while she cooked her supper. She never turned it up past a certain point, the 'third line' she told me. If I went out to sit on my porch, which I often do, I could hear it, but not enough to make out any songs or anything. And she never put the volume any higher.

"But last night about five minutes after she got home, oh, say between eleven forty-five and midnight, the music was suddenly cranked up really loud. It made the windows of that little house shake."

Harmes was staring at her. None of the patrol cops had touched anything, or at least they said. Kelly said the same. The killer must have shut off the stereo, but why?

"Was it on when you woke up this morning?" he asked. "Did you see anyone come or go?"

She shook her head. "No. I saw no one else on the dead-end street; no cars, no people, nothing. Anyway, the stereo suddenly went off around twelve fifteen or so. Just suddenly. The lights were on all night. I just knew something wasn't right. Shannon never left her lights on; just the one on the porch, like she did when she left. You know, to light the door when she got back home."

Harmes took the woman's name and number and gave her his card, promising they would be in touch if they had any more questions. He also encouraged her to give him a call if any more information came to her mind. When they were finished Harmes turned and looked back at the house for the thousandth time. It sounded to him like the guy was already inside when Shannon Helms had arrived home.

He walked back into the house to find the men scrutinizing something high up on the door.

Joe Carter glanced at him. "Looks like a brand-new padlock device, but there is no padlock."

Harmes elbowed between the men and stood on his toes to look at the metal flap and hoop screwed to the door. He took his forefinger and pointed to the area with a screw in it.

"Do you see all the bits of wood?" Now Harmes knelt to the floor. "No sawdust; only tiny bits of wood. This was done by hand, and that tiny little Shannon Helms couldn't have done it. This was just put in. I think she did lock the door. I think she turned on her

music, just like always, and went to the kitchen."
Harmes turned away from the other men and walked
purposefully into the kitchen and dining area.

"Then, I think the killer used the padlock to lock her
in her own home."

He gestured toward the meat still sitting on the
counter in a pool of drying blood. "She likely came in
and took the meat out, and that was when he locked it.
He did it when her back was turned, of course. Mrs.
Catman, the old lady I just spoke to, she said there was
music on last night, loud, just like every other night.
Kelly said she touched nothing in the house, and it was
quiet. The music was turned up crazy-loud for about a
half-hour, according to Mrs. Catman, louder than
Shannon had ever put it before. The killer blared it to
muffle her screams, then turned it down before he left
to keep the neighbors from getting upset or concerned.
He wanted to keep her from being found until
morning."

Harmes looked slowly around the kitchen once
again, then continued. "She tossed her purse on the
table, right where it was found, then got the meat out.
The killer, we assume, was already in the house; I
wouldn't doubt it if he sent the tickets himself just to
get her out of here so he could do whatever he did. He
might even have been watching her while she was
pulling the meat out and putting it on the counter. Now
she needs a pan."

Harmes turned toward the hanging rack of pans over the small island the cooking range was in. "She turned around to get it and there he was. No blood in here, not even the sign of a struggle. No stools knocked over from the island at all. They aren't even pulled out, so she didn't have company. We can probably safely bet that she didn't know the perp. He was a stranger. She tries to run past him, and from the order that we see in the living room, he let her. He was getting off on her panic and fear.

"She tries to get out the door, and even gets the locks unlocked; Kelly Packard said so; she put the key in, but the door was all the way unlocked. But the door won't open for Shannon Helms, and why? Because the perp has padlocked it while she's turned away." Harmes flipped at the lockless loop with his finger. "Yep. He was inside here waiting."

"So what, he chases her down the hall and gets it over with?" Carter asked.

Harmes turned and walked toward the hallway. To the right was Shannon's bedroom; straight ahead was the small bathroom. Down the hall to the left was the back door.

"Nah, I don't think so," he mumbled in reply. He was staring toward the bedroom, then walked two short steps and crossed the threshold. "The blinds were askew like that when we arrived. The bed is made but messy." He went silent for a moment. "I think she ran in here, and I'm pretty sure she was trying to open the window.

The rest of the house is very tidy, but the bedspread is rumpled all up. She was on her knees on that bed trying to get out the window."

Carter shook his head. "But it didn't happen here; no blood in here, boss."

"Nope." It didn't happen in the bedroom, but he could see him standing in the bedroom doorway watching her struggle, maybe even laughing. He crossed the small room and stood at the foot of the bed inspecting the window. With his gloved hands he tried to open it; it wouldn't budge, even in its unlocked state. Then he saw it, and he pointed at it with one gloved finger. "Nailed shut, boys. He knew she wasn't going anywhere, so he watched her struggle. Probably got off on it."

He started out of the room, stopping just long enough to point to a tangled wad of long, blond hair on the dark carpet on the floor. "I think he grabbed her and tried to yank her back as she ran, but that was all he got." As soon as he pointed another officer knelt down to pick up the hair and place it in a bag.

Harmes continued, and as he passed the others he said, "He let her continue past him, even after he grabbed her hair. I think he wanted to do it in the bedroom, but she was too fast for him. She ran to the back... probably thinking she would go out the back door." Harmes reached the area and looked down at the police outline where her body had lain; a pink Columbia jacket was wadded there. "The poor kid tripped and fell, and he was on her like a lion on a zebra. Game over."

When Harmes turned back to his men they were all just staring at the outline too. Everyone was thinking about Harmes' proposed scenario. With each passing second it sounded more and more on track to all of them.

Finally, Carter spoke up. "Sounds good to me, and looks even better. Let's all go with this for now. Let's get to work."

The other men left Harmes standing in the hall, studying the outline. He told them he would catch up with them later, and soon he was the only one in the house. He took his cell from his trouser pocket and used the internet to get the number he was looking for, then tapped it and put the phone to his ear.

After a brief pause upon answer, Harmes said, "Hi. I'm wondering if you can tell me the times for the showings of *Smash Hit*, please?"

Kevin Harmes had decided that he was going to visit the Savoy Multiplex soon and check out a movie.

CHAPTER 9

There had been a time that Monday had been the man's favorite day of the week. He loved his work, and always looked forward to it, no matter how grueling work could be. But now, sitting in the middle of a meeting, listening to a colleague drone on and on, he couldn't help but daydream of Friday.

Friday was the day to look forward to now, now that he had gone ahead and begun the process he had always dreamed of. The process of proving how valuable he really was. How he was the one and only, the very best of all time. The money he made and any recognition he got due to his career had begun to mean nothing to him; he wanted to prove himself to all those who knew the real man... the man he had always been.

He looked at the colleague who was talking, and he offered up a nod every now and then, but he couldn't hear a word the guy was saying. He was high on his thoughts. You see, on Sunday morning he began to plan the Third Act, and he was so eager he could barely sit still. He needed to be viewing the movie and planning accordingly. Didn't these ignorant annoyances in his life understand that sometimes he had other things to do than coddle them?

His mind went back to his pet project and the next act. This was the genius of it: The Third Act would not be taking place in LA. No, he would take it to Sacramento on Friday. He already had a single ticket sent to a girl there, a girl he had hand-picked to help make his masterpiece fully tangible.

"What do you think of that approach?"

He snapped out of it for a second. "Um, I agree. I'm just not sure…"

"You haven't heard a word I said, have you?" The man stood angrily and grabbed his coat from the chair next to him. "I'll be in touch. The only thing you have going for you right now is the fact that your numbers are astronomical. Snap out of it!"

The man left his office, and he sat back in his chair. Oh, well; life goes on. He had another meeting in ten minutes, and it was far more important than the bull he had just endured. Frankly, he didn't need any of them.

When he got home he would go over the footage to be 'reproduced' in Sacramento, and he would do it until he got a bit of relief. The killing was the only thing that could do it for him, but the planning and watching sure gave him excitement as well.

The ego and power were a couple of very powerful aphrodisiacs.

Detective Kevin Harmes had sat in his car staring straight ahead. It was nearly nine thirty at night, and he had been parked at the Savoy Multiplex for some time. Kevin had been out of the movie for nearly forty minutes. The fact of the matter was that his mind was racing as he sat there, and it just hadn't been safe for him to drive yet.

Jennifer Schmidt, the witness to the first murder, had been right. Lauren Connors' murder was not just similar to the first murder scene in the film; it was eerily identical. So much so, in fact, that Harmes was nauseous.

But that was only the beginning.

The second murder, by the time it hit the screen, nearly made him hurl right there in his seat. Shannon Helms' murder lined up to it exactly, and his theory about the order of things which took place in her home was dead on as well, or at least it was in the movie. The difference was that the victim in the movie, who resembled Helms greatly, was killed in the bedroom. Shannon's killer wasn't able to stop her as it was done in the movie; she had slipped out of his grasp and run for the back door. Unfortunately for the pretty paralegal she was taken down there.

As he sat there in his car at the Savoy he knew one thing, and he knew it in both his mind and his heart: there was a serial killer in Los Angeles. He no longer believed it was just some high school kid; similar killings would have been happening with the release of every horror film. No, Harmes thought that whoever was doing this had something to say, though he didn't know what. He was also sure that he was a big movie fan.

∞

Excited for Sacramento, the man stepped from the steamy hotel bathroom, one towel around his waist and another draped over his head, leaving his face and chest showing. He crossed the room and poured a snifter of brandy and took a long drink before filling it again. He always felt spectacular after getting rid of the excitement he got when reviewing the murder scenes. It refreshed him and made him look forward to the relief of carrying out yet another 'live' scene.

Sacramento also turned him on. He'd had some pretty good times partying with college friends when they traveled there in younger years, and everywhere he looked brought back good memories. Well, sooner rather than later he'd be making another one.

The killing would be based on the third murder in *Smash Hit*, and it would also be the Third Act in his masterpiece. He would use the next several days to get up to par, and on Friday he would begin the making of the Third Act.

His co-star in the Third Act would be a cute little Goth chick that had an apartment in the Village. He knew her from the restaurant he frequented in LA, and that is where he saw her and her boyfriend at first. The kid worked there during the week and then went to stay with her on the weekends. She had visited her boyfriend at work a couple of times, and she would be perfect for the part he wanted her to play.

He had, once again, watched the third murder more times that he could count, and it played effortlessly in his mind at all times, but that wouldn't stop him from obsessing further. Perfect. Initially, he was going to send Victim Three one ticket, but he changed his mind; better to let her take Junior. He could steer all eyes to this kid, and it would be a genius 'smoke and mirrors' ploy, a side-game for amusement, if you will.

So, he purchased two tickets, popped them into an envelope, and wrote: 'For Kimber Ryan: Have fun, kids!' on the front. Next he slid it through the slot at the coffee house where she worked, under the cover of night. He'd have his eyes on them. He was ready, no matter the circumstances. He would knock the boyfriend, Davis Reed, out cold. He would kill the girl, put the knife in the kid's hand, cover him with blood, and sit back and watch the fun. They would all freak, ha ha. It would be just like in the movie.

That was why the Fourth Act would not be found until Monday or Tuesday, whenever he decided to anonymously report a dead body. By then he would be in San Diego, putting the Fifth Act together. It was too perfect, and it was way too much fun.

Flinging his towel across the room, he drained his drink and lay naked on his bed; time to check out the news and find out how the cops in LA were coming along.

∞

Kevin Harmes was a mess.

He sat behind his desk in silence, the only light in the room a desk lamp that cast a surreal orb of light over his binder and strewn file. His mind was on the last few days, and what he had discovered during that time. None of it felt good. Now it was already Thursday night; not another murder had taken place since Shannon Helms'. Harmes was convinced he was on a far better track theoretically. Because no one else had been murdered, even though *Smash Hit* was still at the top of the box office charts, he figured that maybe it had been a kid or kids all along, and that they had gotten both bored with their little game, and scared by it. If he had been correct, and it was in fact a serial killer, certainly another murder would have come to light by now. Yes, he thought to himself, I need to start looking harder at high school kids in the area again, just to be sure. I just want to be positive that it's not some psycho kid before I move on my next hunch.

He reached up and shut off his desk lamp. Time to head home. Tomorrow would be Friday, and he could get a fresh start knocking on doors and visiting the high school attended by the first two victims, Lauren Connors and her boyfriend, Chad Bryan.

Kevin Harmes left work in silence, a nagging feeling in his stomach that he just couldn't place.

R.W.K. Clark

CHAPTER 10

On Saturday morning the man was up bright and early. He wanted to watch the news. He wanted to see what they had to say about the murder of the barista, Kimber Ryan. The truth was, he could barely sit still.

Her killing had been simple. Her apartment was in the basement of an old brownstone in the Village, and the place was rock-solid and virtually soundproof. He didn't care if he was heard anyway; rumor had it at the coffee house where the couple hung out, the pair had loud, crazy parties all the time, and neighbors never complained. He had nothing to worry about.

He had hidden in a small coat closet next to the door, and when they came back and locked themselves in he just popped out and slammed a brick into the back of the kid's head. Putting out Davis Reed was fun, but he wasn't done yet.

He made her tie the kid up; then he tied her up. He waited until the kid woke, then proceeded to mutilate and torture the silly little Goth chick until she passed out from the pain. After that it wasn't fun, and he stabbed her somewhere around fifteen times with his knife.

The kid was on the floor going nuts, crying and trying to scream through the duct tape.

"I'm gonna untie you, but on one condition: you need to grab onto her body and hold it tight. Close your eyes and count to sixty, and I'll be gone. If you don't count to sixty I'm gonna find you and finish you off too, and it will be much worse."

He untied Davis Reed, and the kid ran to his girlfriend's lifeless body. He lay next to her on the floor sobbing and embracing her tightly; her blood was all over him. He had stood there and reveled in the sight for several minutes before speaking.

"Close your eyes and start counting!"

The boy did it, and at the count of fifteen he had run out the door and stolen away into the night, but not before tossing the knife on the floor beside them. Time to report a murder.

That had been just hours ago, and it had been heaven.

∞

"Good morning, and welcome to your six o'clock morning news; this is Kyla Henry. An anonymous phone tip led police to a grisly scene in the Village early this morning. At four a.m. police responded to the call to find the mutilated body of Kimber Ryan, 25. Her boyfriend, Davis Reed of Los Angeles, was taken into custody at the scene. At the current time Reed is being held for questioning, and the department will not comment on whether charges are pending. Miss Ryan's family has been notified of her death. In other news…"

∞

The man muted the television. He was aggravated; what was that? It didn't take up two minutes? But he stewed for a brief time. The crime in Sacramento obviously hadn't been connected to those in LA yet. That would be done by Detective Harmes. He was a smart one; he would soon see the pattern and recognize exactly what he was trying to create with these acts. He was the first on the case, and Harmes was the one he wanted to finally catch him, if indeed Harmes could.

"The Third Act," he said with a smile. "Time for the fourth."

∞

Detective Harmes sat at his desk, his stomach in knots. He should have known; he should have known from the very start that the murders were not going to be run of the mill. So far as he could tell, the state of California had a pretty major problem. The state had a serial killer on its hands.

He found out about the murder in Sacramento on the news while he was getting ready for work. He hadn't even eaten breakfast, but that didn't stop him from throwing back his coffee, and as soon as he had he made a beeline for his office. He arrived to find more than twenty messages on his voicemail, each one from a citizen, and each one telling him how the murders sounded like the movie. The most frightening thing of all was that no one seemed scared by it; the box office numbers showed that the flick was still going through the roof, and they were on the rise.

Sacramento had a suspect in custody. A kid named Davis Reed had been found at the scene of the last murder with blood all over him. All the press had released about the kid so far was that his main residence was in LA, but he stayed weekends with the victim in Sacramento. They had other information, but police hadn't yet released it. It didn't matter to Harmes what they had; he wasn't buying that the Reed kid was the killer. No, the killer was exacting, and he would never let himself be found, nor would he kill someone so close to him. Of those things Harmes was sure.

An hour ago he had a phone conference with the lead investigator on the Sacramento case. Harmes had shared with him all of the details of his own cases, and he had tried to drive his 'copycat killer' theory home, but the guy wasn't buying it. He had been convinced that the Reed kid was the killer, and as far as he was concerned it was a waste of time to talk to Harmes at all.

Then, five minutes ago he got a return call from the guy. Turns out that Davis Reed couldn't have been the killer because he was in Sacramento every weekend, and that fact was easily verified. The killings took place on

Friday and Saturday, at least so far. He had been released, and the cop was beginning to become convinced. Upon agreement, both locations released to the press that they recommended that the movie *Smash Hit* be avoided in all places it was being shown, and that patrons should not attend any showing. They wouldn't know until that night whether or not anyone would listen.

If the killer stayed true to form, there would be another murder. It was Saturday, after all. Harmes guessed it would take place in Sacramento. It seemed the killer, or the Box Office Butcher, liked to hop to keep them moving. But it was pretty early in the game to know for sure.

Right now it was a waiting game, and it was in the stage that Harmes desperately hated. It was a matter of another body turning up. The fourth killing in the movie involved a young invalid, a paraplegic who lived alone in a small house by the ocean. The actual murder is a masterpiece of horror, as the handicapped girl flees from her attacker for fifteen minutes before he tears the life from her already-damaged body. The thought of finding someone like this made Harmes want to puke yet again, but he fully expected it to happen, and it would happen today.

He began to try to find paraplegics in Sacramento who owned or rented houses. It would be a long process, and it was one he had to go through alone because no one would buy into his theories. But he set to work, hoping to get lucky sooner than later.

Deep in his heart, Kevin Harmes knew he was right about the Box Office Butcher.

CHAPTER 11

Smash Hit was sold out in all of the area theaters, but the truth of the matter was that Claire Hudson couldn't have cared less. She wasn't a fan of the horror genre, and when her friends had asked her to go with them that evening, she'd declined. She had been watching the news, and something about the entire situation had her petrified.

No, she would stay safely at home and have a warm meal, and maybe she would even watch a nice, peaceful romance. Besides, it was always a pain for her to get her wheelchair around big mobs of people, and that was what the theaters were full of with a hit movie like this playing. She was more than content to put *Smash Hit* all the way out of her mind.

The phone rang.

"Hello?" Claire answered sweetly.

"Claire, it's Bobbie." Her best friend's chipper voice met her ear and made her smile. "I know you said you didn't want to go tonight, but I thought I would ask again."

Claire smiled to herself and shook her head slightly. "Bobbie, I'm just tired. And besides, you know how I feel about horror movies. I'm gonna pass, hon."

"Well, okay," her friend replied. "We're getting ready to leave now. Do you want me to stop and check on you after? We could have some wine."

"Actually, I'm going to watch a chick flick and turn in early. You just have fun, okay?"

The girls hung up and Claire aimed her motorized wheelchair for the kitchen. She wanted to make a simple chicken breast with stuffed mushrooms and asparagus on the side. Cooking was the one true passion she still had since the accident, and she was so thankful she still had the use of her arms. It was going to be a good night, and she was looking forward to indulging her hobby of cooking and being alone.

∞

The man sat on a slight hill about one hundred yards out in the back of Claire Hudson's house. His binoculars were focused on the back of the woman's house, which consisted of windows and a pair of sliding glass doors with ramps coming off of them. But the fact that he could easily watch her was one of the reasons she was chosen.

Claire hadn't seen the movie, nor would she. In *Smash Hit*, the fourth victim was also a paraplegic. The young woman fit the bill perfectly, and now, tonight, he would put her out of her misery. No human could be happy confined to a wheelchair, in his opinion, so she would fulfill his next act perfectly, she would also receive the reward of entering the afterlife. Perfect.

He spied on her as she tooled around her kitchen; she was beginning to prepare her dinner. Just like in the movie, he would wait until it was finished and she had started eating before he began his little cat and mouse game. Soon, Claire Hudson would be famous, and he would have completed yet another act in his masterpiece. By the time he was finished there wouldn't be a killer known to man who had been able to accomplish what he was doing other than him. He was making the perfect series of killings, and none of it was on a whim.

The sun was beginning to go down, and it was getting a bit more difficult for him to see through the binoculars. He put them down and leaned back against a large rock. He inhaled deeply and turned his eyes to the sky. It was promising to be a beautiful night, and Claire Hudson would make everything even more wonderful than it already was.

He thought about his little foiled plan involving Davis Reed. He had thought that Reed would be held by the Sacramento police for several days, but he let it slip his mind that Reed was actually in Sacramento, not LA, during the first two killings. Since he had been released, there was no need to wait to call police to report Claire once she was dead. Their focus was already back on the true facts, so he would report her immediately after arriving in San Diego tomorrow morning.

It was nothing more than a tiny glitch, and it certainly wouldn't prove to stop him from carrying out the things he needed to do to successfully complete his goals.

∞

Kevin Harmes was feeling relieved.

He had managed to convince the Sacramento police that their killer was basing the murders on those featured in *Smash Hit*, and now the news was actively encouraging the public to avoid the film at all costs. The problem now was that as soon as the news made the announcements every ticket in the US seemed to be sold out.

It appeared the public was actually getting off on the fact that there was some sicko running around, and they were willing to take their chances.

But the country had another problem as well. Kids, posing as the Box Office Butcher, were killing people all over the place. Copycats of the copycat was all they were, and they were getting caught easily. According to reports seven such murders had taken place so far: one each in Maryland, Minnesota, Washington State, Texas, and Alabama. Two had been reported in Florida. It was a massive mess, and neither Harmes nor any of his men could believe the repercussions that were playing out.

But Kevin Harmes didn't have time to worry about that. Right now he was driving on the freeway in Sacramento. His investigation had turned up two women who were paraplegics in the Sacramento area who lived alone. One had a small, inherited house in the suburbs; the other had one on the side of a cliff overlooking the Pacific. He intended to visit them both in hopes of catching the Box Office Butcher in his tracks. His first stop would be the home of Christina Harrington, the paraplegic in the 'burbs.

He reached down and turned his radio up, but he didn't hear the song or its words. Kevin Harmes couldn't get the murders off his mind, and he was going nuts thinking a helpless handicapped person was going to get it next. He was sure that if he could get to the suspected victim on time he could stop everything.

He pulled into the fast lane and punched the accelerator; he needed to get moving, and he needed to do it now.

R.W.K. Clark

CHAPTER 12

The jet airliner streaked through the night sky like a knife cutting through butter. The man sat with his seat slightly reclined, his head back on his tiny pillow, and his eyes loosely closed. It had been one heck of a night at Claire Hudson's; everything had gone so perfectly that he felt a deep, twisted sense of gratitude that he couldn't quite identify.

He had sat in the back, in the dark, watching the pretty red-haired paraplegic as she wheeled around her kitchen and prepared her food. He could see her through her lit windows, but just slightly. The distance made it difficult, and his shoulders and neck had begun hurting from using the binoculars, but he was able to easily tell when she took her plate of food and set it on her table beside the lit candle and glass of white wine.

That had been his signal. He had stood up and stretched out, then proceeded to put his mask on and make his way through the darkness of her backyard toward her home and the open window in her office, the window he had opened himself when she had been out earlier in the day. He slipped in, making little to no sound, and waited five minutes before leaving the room and approaching the kitchen, where he stood in silence and watched her eat until her plate was nearly clean.

"How was it?" he had asked her as she drained her glass of wine.

Claire had swung her head around, a stricken and panicked look on her face. He'd simply watched the terror come over her face, and he'd reveled in the sound of her whimpers as she had started to cry. It hadn't taken long for the young woman to hit the joystick on her wheelchair and race toward him. He had expected this, and he had dodged out of her way just before she had run over his toes; it had made him laugh.

For the next twenty minutes he chased her around the small house, laughing and commenting on how she had no escape, how he was there to 'take her pain away'. It was so much fun that he hoped it would never end, but end it did when her chair hit a shoe and she flew, face first, onto the floor in the living room.

He couldn't do her there, though. In the movie the girl in the wheelchair had been killed in her office, so he grabbed Claire by her arms and dragged her through the house and into the small spare room that served as her study. She cried and screamed and swung blindly at him as he removed her pants; he knew she thought he was going to rape her.

"Don't worry," he said. "Raping you is the very last thing on my mind. I intend to kill you, but I have to leave a message."

At that point she began to scream herself hoarse, and he simply let her do so, humming the entire time. Once her pants were around her ankles he pulled his knife out of his pocket and held it up over her face; it silenced her almost immediately. He even turned it around so she could see the light reflecting off of it. Her screams turned instantly to silent sobs.

"I know you are paralyzed from the waist down, so I will make sure to carve where you cannot feel."

He began. He wanted the words to be clear and easy to read. Even though she could feel nothing Claire cried like a baby as he set about his task. When he was finished he took hold of her tear-covered face and made her look him in the eyes.

"I'll make it quick," he whispered.

He did. He plunged his knife into her lower belly, right above her pelvic bone, and he drew the blade upward toward her face, cutting her open from bottom to top. Her mouth gaped open silently and her eyes were wide with disbelief as it happened. She had gone into shock several minutes before.

He wasn't satisfied until he was able to see her intestines. When he could he stood and stared down at her limp body until he could see that she was no longer breathing. Then he felt her pulse; there was none, and he stood once again with a smile on his face. He looked down at the words he had carved, one word per thigh:

'Fourth Act'.

So, with this part of his job complete, he simply left by means of one of the sliding glass doors off the kitchen. He took a trail down to his rental car, which was parked in a pull off along the beach. Once he was in the car he removed his mask and began to drive in the direction of the airport; his packed bags were in the trunk, and he had a flight to catch to San Diego. He would call and anonymously report Claire's body in the morning. For now he was content to toss his bloody knife out the car window and over a cliff as he drove.

San Diego, here I come to carry out the Fifth Act, and yes, the Sixth. The Final Act in his masterpiece.

∞

Harmes had a panicky feeling in his stomach. He was driving like a madman to get to the home of Claire Hudson. His first stop had been at the suburbs, where he had paid a brief visit to Christina Harrington, the other paraplegic on his list.

As soon as he had pulled up to her home his heart had sunk; the houses on the street were very close together, and it seemed all the windows were lit and full of family activities. Doubt tugged at his heart right away. In the movie the fourth victim lived in a home that was far from all others. Well, it wouldn't hurt to meet the woman anyway.

He had knocked, and as soon as Christina Harrington answered he knew he was way off. She was in her fifties; the movie victim had been in her twenties.

After a brief visit he learned that she had been in a bus accident. In the movie the victim had been paralyzed while driving.

Harmes gave the woman a brief but heartfelt apology for bothering her, and he left quickly. Now he was on his way to the home of one Claire Hudson, but no matter how fast he drove he felt as if he couldn't get there fast enough. He felt the familiar tugging of instinct: Claire was likely the Box Office Butcher's next victim. Kevin Harmes had sincerely messed up by going to see Christina Harrington first.

When he finally got up the cliff and pulled into the young lady's driveway he saw all the lights on in her home. This gave him hope; maybe he wasn't too late after all. Maybe he had gotten there in time to stop the killer.

He pulled the car up on the gravel next to a large conversion van with handicap license plates on it. After shutting off his own vehicle, Harmes climbed out and made his way to the house. It was totally aglow with lighting, including the porch light. Barely-audible music was wafting through one of the windows, but he couldn't make out the song or even the type of music it was. Soon he was on the porch, knocking, and he glanced at his watch: nine forty-five.

His first knock brought no response, so Kevin knocked again, this time with more persistence. "Miss Hudson, it's Detective Harmes with the Los Angeles police. Could I have a word with you, please?"

After waiting another minute his concern began to grow. Kevin looked around the property; he could see no houses anywhere near Claire's, so he left the porch and looked into the darkness that covered the backyard: no lights or houses in sight.

Back on the porch he knocked again, but this time he used his fist and pounded on the door. "Miss Hudson! Police!"

But in his soul Kevin knew she was not going to be answering, and he doubted very highly that it was because she wasn't at home. Her van was in the drive and all of the lights were on, not to mention the fact that there were no nearby houses that she could simply wheel her chair to, not without going down the steep drive, which ran up and down a cliff, basically.

Kevin reached down and rattled the doorknob, but it was locked. "Oh, heck," he muttered as he took his cell and dialed the number to the Sacramento Police. He wanted to go in, but he couldn't do so without cause, and being out of his jurisdiction put him out of his element entirely.

"Hi, this is Detective Kevin Harmes, with the LAPD," he said into the phone. "I need police backup at a residence in your jurisdiction right away, please."

The police receptionist began to give him trouble right away, asking if the matter was official or casual. Then she wanted to know what he was doing conducting an investigation out of his jurisdiction. Finally, Kevin snapped and requested to speak with the duty officer right away. Once he got that man on the phone and explained the situation, he was promised backup right away.

It didn't take long for his backup to arrive. Two cars pulled in with their lights going furiously, but they had their sirens off. Three patrolmen and an officer in a suit approached him quickly, the suit holding his hand out as if to shake Kevin's.

"I'm Detective Arnold, lead on the latest suspected Box Office Butcher killing here in Sacramento," the man said as they shook. "What do you have here, Detective Harmes, and what are you doing in my city?"

Kevin related quickly the reason for his visit to Claire Hudson's home. He filled in the detective on his suspicions regarding the murders in LA, and he told them that he was receiving no response from the resident of the house. The newly-arrived officers grew immediately suspicious, and Kevin was relieved to see that it seemed they all believed what he had to say.

"All right," Arnold told the uniformed officers. "Let's try to get an answer; if we can't we'll go on in, guns drawn."

Armed and at the door, the uniforms knocked twice. After that they wasted no time in kicking the door in and beginning the search for Claire Hudson. Unfortunately, she was found in near record time, especially after observing her power wheelchair turned over on the living room floor.

She was lying on the floor of what appeared to be a home office. Her stomach was torn open and was gaping so dramatically that her intestines and other innards were clearly visible; one officer even ran for the door to vomit. Another called for an ambulance right away, informing dispatch that the victim was DOA.

"No," Detective Arnold said. "This is a nightmare. Someone is killing according to this deranged movie."

Kevin turned to him. "You've seen it?"

"I went to the first showing this evening," he replied. "After it got to be the word that the murders were based on the film I thought it wise that I check it out. I was in agreement, but I was hoping I was wrong. This just confirms it all."

Kevin could barely nod; he felt like he might die from the guilt of not coming to Claire Hudson's home first.

"Look at her legs," Arnold said.

Kevin knelt down next to the girl's blood-covered corpse. "I saw it: 'The Fourth Act'. The sicko is making a real-life movie, you know."

The officers went outside to wait for the crime scene investigators and the ambulance. Kevin Harmes and Detective Ralph Arnold talked and compared notes while they waited. It seemed that Arnold was just getting up to speed on many things that Kevin already either suspected or knew already.

"So, from what I see the guy is just copying a movie," he said. "How can we be sure it's the same perp?"

Kevin turned to the man. "Every killing is identical in almost every detail, with the exception being the sick little 'Act' notes," he said. "Even the first killing was eerily identical, and it happened on opening night. I have to tell you, I suspect a very specific individual here."

"And who would that be?" Arnold pressed.

Harmes cleared his throat. "Whoever this sicko is, I'm willing to bet he is one of the insiders on this sick flick."

R.W.K. Clark

CHAPTER 13

Regarding the movie *Smash Hit*, things had gotten completely out of control all over the United States.

People were assaulting others everywhere, and murders and attempted murders were growing by the numbers. It seemed to be some kind of sick fad for people to dress like the killer in the film and stalk and kill victims. It took police a major amount of time to separate copycats from the real Box Office Butcher, but the fact that the real one left his little 'Act' notes, something that hadn't been released to the media, made their job a little bit easier.

Another thing was that *Smash Hit* was drawing more people for viewing than any other movie in history. They flocked in great hordes to see it, not once or twice, but over and over again. Each and every night a scattering of victims would pop up all over the place, attacked, beaten, and even killed in manners which aped the movie on the big screen. It got to the point that police everywhere wanted the movie shut down for the good of the public, and they wanted it done right away.

Detective Kevin Harmes, Detective Ralph Arnold, and several other detectives from all over discussed meeting with the Federal Communications Commission and obtaining an order to have the movie pulled from all theaters. The week following Claire Hudson's murder was the worst ever for excessive attacks and killings, and on Tuesday three FCC agents met with Harmes, Arnold, and several other police officials who flew to the Los Angeles area to request that the movie be stopped.

The meeting proved a bit fruitful. The FCC would present the request to the federal court for review. Even if it couldn't be stopped right away, it could be temporarily frozen for up to three days while the court considered permanent removal. Because it was an issue of public safety the FCC was almost sure it wouldn't be an issue.

But that was before the director and producer of the movie, Miles March himself, was served with legal paperwork on Tuesday evening while at his LA office.

∞

"Mr. March, you must be aware of the circumstances being created by *Smash Hit*." The man speaking was Agent Tom Burgess of the FCC. He was seated across from March's desk, along with his partner, Vic Rimes, and a federal investigator named Kenneth Bogs. "We would have asked you to the initial meeting this morning, but you were out of town. The fact that you flew back for an emergency board meeting of Milestone Pictures, your company, made it possible for us to come and speak to you face to face. Thank you for seeing us."

Miles March listened to the man patiently, his fingers steepled under his chin and his concentration firmly set on what was being said. "I received word of your intention to pull *Smash Hit* while I was on location for my next film. The one reason I flew in was for a meeting called to discuss what you are trying to do. You understand that I cannot willingly agree to such a request."

Vic Rimes spoke. "Mr. March, you do understand that countless people are dying, and all of the attacks are based on the murders in your film. Your company, Milestone Pictures, and all who worked on making *Smash Hit* will be coming under investigation. It is in your best interest to cease and desist without court order."

"In my best interest?" March began to laugh loudly, almost hysterical. "You know *Smash Hit* is currently making more money than any movie ever. To close it down would be to rob myself and all involved in its creation. How could pulling it be in my best interest?"

Tom Burgess took a deep breath and sat back in his chair. "Mr. March, a federal court judge will at least put a three-day hold on it until it can be reviewed more carefully, but chances are you will lose if you decide to defy our request. Think of the money you will lose then. It's best to quit while you're ahead, don't you think?"

Miles March stood and began to pace. After a moment he said, "I won't be bullied by you or any other government employee, do you understand? You should know that my board and all who are involved agree with me."

"You will be virtually responsible for anyone who dies after this meeting if you do not comply, sir," said Vic Rimes, his voice sharp with frustration. "I would think a man of your standing in the industry would want anything but that."

Miles March walked to his desk and opened the top drawer, then pulled out a card and handed it over to Rimes. "Here you go: my attorneys. You go ahead and give them a call in the morning and see what they have to say about the issue. I will fight this, and I will hire every single powerhouse lawyer in the United States. You will not dictate to me when, how, or why I exercise my Constitutional rights, so I guess I'll see you in court." He sat back down at his desk. "Good evening, gentlemen."

The two FCC agents and the federal investigator simply stared across the desk at him, shocked for a moment. They simply couldn't believe the lack of heart and soul in the man. Finally, Investigator Kenneth Bogs spoke.

"Fine, Mr. March. Have it any way you want it," he said as he fished his own card out of his pocket and tossed it on March's desk. "In the meantime, while we wait for all of this to be sorted out, if you think of anyone from your cast or crew who may be suspect, please, give me a call. At the current time we are fairly convinced that our killer is one of yours, and it would halt the pulling of *Smash Hit* if we can catch the killer."

The three men rose and said their goodbyes while March simply stared at them. Once they were gone he picked up Bogs' card and looked at it for a long moment before tossing it back down and picking up the phone. It was definitely time to call his lawyers; the feds could kiss his butt.

Miles March's attorney was Asa Kennedy of Kennedy, Locke, and Garling, which just happened to be one of Hollywood's most prestigious and successful firms. The attorneys at Kennedy, Locke, and Garling won every case they put their hands on, and they had the power to draw in assistance from any other firm they desired. Someone in showbiz could easily get out of a murder rap, if that was needed. Those lawyers could convince the court that the D.A. himself was the killer. But all he needed them for was to stop the government from pulling *Smash Hit* out of theaters, and they were just the firm to get the job done.

He quickly dialed Asa's cell number, which was answered after two rings.

"Asa Kennedy."

Miles smiled and cleared his throat. "Asa, it's Miles March. I need to see you as soon as possible. I've got a bunch of feds breathing down my neck; they want to pull *Smash Hit*."

He scheduled an appointment for the next morning with Asa, and hung up the phone just as a light knock came on his office door. Who could that be this time of the evening? This was the kind of stuff that wore him out and frustrated him. He had more important things to do.

"Enter."

A handsome young man stepped into Miles' office, a brilliant white smile flashing and blue eyes shining from too much coke. It was Cory Caine, his lead actor from *Smash Hit*. Miles sighed and forced a smile.

"Cory," he greeted the young man. "What do you need? It's a little late, isn't it?"

Cory closed the door behind him. "Sorry to bother you, Chief," he began. "I just got back from Sacramento; I was visiting my mother. Crazy, all the stuff happening because of *Smash Hit*, huh?"

Miles nodded. "And?"

"Well, I'm getting ready to head to San Diego to meet up with my girl," he continued. "I just wanted to make sure you didn't need me for interviews or anything because of the craziness."

Miles shook his head. "San Diego, huh? How long will you be there?"

Cory shrugged. "A week or so."

"Hmmm." Miles studied his star. "Is your mom okay? I didn't even know you were in Sacramento. When did you get back?"

"Just now. I went last Thursday; she wanted to spend some time with her big star son, you know what I mean?"

"Yeah." Miles continued to study Cory, his mind racing. Sacramento? "Are you keeping up with your promotional appearances?"

"Absolutely, Chief," the kid replied.

Miles March offered Cory a tired smile and picked up a pen as if to do some work. "Sounds good. I have your cell; if anything comes up I'll be sure to call you, okay? Just make sure you answer every time. Too much is going on, and the cops mentioned wanting to question the cast and crew."

"No problem," he said. "See you in a week or so otherwise, Miles."

Miles nodded once again. "Sounds good. Travel safely."

Cory Caine left his office and Miles stared at the door for several moments after it closed. Los Angeles for the release of *Smash Hit*, then to Sacramento since last Thursday? Could Cory Caine, one of the most up and coming stars of the day, be the Box Office Butcher?

Miles picked up Kenneth Bogs' card. It gave his office number as well as a number for his cellular phone. Miles dialed the cell number and waited. Bogs answered after two rings.

"Investigator Bogs?" he said. "This is Miles March. I think I may know of someone you should look at for your Box Office Butcher."

CHAPTER 14

The sun was shining beautifully when Kevin Harmes was driving to work Thursday morning. For all of the violent murders, and all of the insanity being produced by *Smash Hit*, he was in a good mood, which was pretty rare for Harmes. Whether it was the gorgeous weather or the fact that he believed the feds were going to pull *Smash Hit* either that day or the next that made him feel cheerful he didn't know. But he did feel good.

Once he was at the station he strolled casually to his office, whistling as he went. Just outside of his office, the other detective who had been dabbling in the Box Office Butcher case stopped him. He didn't look nearly as cheerful as Harmes felt.

"Kevin, you have some messages," the man began. "The first I took myself: it was from the federal investigator, Kenneth Bogs. He says he has a suspect, the lead actor in *Smash Hit*, Cory Caine. According to him the director, Miles March, tipped them off that Caine may be the Butcher."

"Really?" Harmes unlocked his office door and jerked his head, motioning for Carter to come inside.

Carter nodded and took a seat across the desk from Kevin. "Yeah. He wants you to call him ASAP to discuss it so you can interview Caine yourself. That's the good news."

Kevin was jotting down everything Carter was saying, but the last bit caused him to stop mid-sentence and look up at his colleague with a knit brow. "Good news?"

"Yeah," Carter replied slowly. "I'm afraid there is bad news as well. *Smash Hit* will not be pulled from theaters."

Kevin was immediately in shock. The thought that the FCC was not going to pull the movie, with all that was happening, was inconceivable to him. He stared at Carter for a moment, stumped as to what he should say. He simply couldn't believe that any court of law would allow a movie to continue to play when there were such violent and extenuating circumstances surrounding it.

"Are you sure?" he asked.

Joe Carter nodded, the look on his face both solemn and filled with disgust. "I'm serious. A closed-door hearing was held, and the judge ruled that it is not the fault of Milestone Pictures that someone is running around offing people according to the plot of one of their movies. Bottom line, end of story. Theaters were notified already concerning the ruling. If you ask me, it helped matters that the head of the company has gazillions of dollars; he probably had every court officer involved tucked neatly away in his pocket."

Harmes took a deep breath and gave a lengthy sigh as his mind tried to wrap around the information. "I guess I had better focus on heading to Milestone Pictures. Hopefully our perp is milling around there someplace."

"Yeah," Carter agreed. "And I'd get moving if I were you. There're rumors that the feds are considering stepping in, and if they do that means our investigation is finished."

Kevin Harmes didn't hesitate to stand up and head for the door. "Come with me, Joe," he said. "Time to visit the studio."

∞

Kevin Harmes and Joe Carter sat in a plush waiting area outside the office of Milestone Pictures president and founder, Miles March. He wasn't in right then, but according to his secretary he was on his way. Kevin felt lucky to have arrived when he did; March had been out of town on business, and would be in his LA office for a couple of hours before jet-setting to another film location.

They had been waiting about an hour when the man himself came striding into the area. He wore an Italian suit that probably cost more than Harmes' tiny house, and the look on his face reeked of smug attitude and ego. At first he took no notice of the officers, but walked past his secretary as if she weren't even there.

"Mr. March, these men are here to see you," the woman said timidly, as though she were afraid to even speak to the man.

Miles March stopped dead in his tracks and turned to the two men. He looked at them, but spoke to his secretary as if they weren't even there. "Do these men have an appointment? You know how my schedule is."

Kevin and Joe Carter both stood, as if on cue, and flashed their badges at the man. "Mr. March, I'm Detective Harmes with the LAPD, and this is my associate, Detective Carter. We need to have a word with you, please."

Miles flashed a brilliant white smile. "I really don't have a lot of time," he said. "But step into my office for now. I'm assuming this is in regard to the *Smash Hit* scandal?"

Kevin nodded as he put his badge back in his jacket. "Can we talk in your office?"

The suit nodded, a thoughtful look in his eyes. "Sure. I expected the police to come eventually. Follow me."

He turned on his heel, both detectives right behind him. When he had opened his office door he paused and held it open for Harmes and Carter. "Have a seat, gentlemen. Can I get you anything to drink? Coffee? Water?"

"No, thanks," Harmes replied for them both as Miles March closed the door. "So, Mr. March, what's your take on the murders?"

March took a seat at his massive oak desk and sat back casually. "Well, I must say that all of it is shocking, to say the least. I would have never thought that one of my horror films would spark such a… movement, but the facts speak for themselves."

Both Harmes and Carter exchanged a glance. "Movement?" Harmes repeated. "That's an odd way to put it."

March smirked and clucked slightly. "I guess what I mean is that I never thought *Smash Hit* would have such a powerful influence on a member of the audience."

Harmes studied the man. "With that being said, have you considered that perhaps it would be in everyone's best interest to pull the movie from theaters, at least temporarily?"

"Detective, it has been determined that I don't need to do that at all." Miles March sat forward, a steely look in his eye that didn't match the smile he was giving them. "Right now *Smash Hit* is bringing in an astronomical amount of money, and the loss we would incur cannot be measured. The murders are a bit of… bad luck, should I say? For the victims, mostly, but for me they are turning out to be quite the cash cow. I will not be pulling the film."

Both detectives could just stare. The level of the man's greed and lack of compassion was almost sickening. Harmes knew, without a doubt, that he would not be able to change the film executive's mind.

"Well," he said, resigned. "Next on the question list would be whether or not you have anyone who worked on the movie's cast or crew that you may have thought was odd, maybe a little obsessive about the story line? Anyone you may suspect would be capable of a crime like the murders?"

Miles March's face relaxed a bit and he began to stare off toward the massive picture window, but he wasn't paying attention to the city lights the office overlooked. "Maybe," he muttered. "I mentioned this to Kenneth Bogs, but after second thought... no, it couldn't be."

Carter flashed a look at Harmes and asked, "You have someone in mind?"

March stood up and began strolling slowly around his office. "Actually, I do. One of my cast members, and I have to say now that I am thinking about it there were many strange, off-color things he did during filming."

Kevin Harmes didn't waste a second. He fished his small notebook and pen out of his jacket, flipped the book open, and poised his pen to begin writing.

"What's this cast member's name?" he asked.

March snapped back to attention. "Cory... Cory Caine. He was my male lead in *Smash Hit*. He played your run-of-the-mill boyfriend, but he winds up being the killer in the end."

Kevin was jotting things down as quickly as he could. "What kind of 'off-color' things are you referring to?"

"Well," March began as he sat back down. "He always had his nose in the script, trying to 'make the scene more believable', as he would put it. To a director and producer that is typically just annoying; actors aren't welcome to give their opinions in these areas, at least, not with me."

Kevin looked up and studied the man for another moment. "More believable?"

"As a matter of fact, he wanted to 'ad lib' the murder scenes to throw off those playing the victims," he continued. "So their fear and screams would be more believable. And he would literally argue with me about it."

Harmes quickly took notes and looked back at Miles March, whose wheels were now turning to the point that it could be seen on his face. He sat forward suddenly, his mouth agape, his lips moving as though he were trying to form words. After a moment he pulled himself together.

"I just talked to him the other day," March said, then he met Kevin's gaze. "He had just gotten back from Sacramento, and he was preparing to leave again... for San Diego, I think he said."

Now Kevin and Joe Carter looked at each other with stricken looks. If Cory Caine was the killer, and it sounded like he might be from his travels and attitudes, he could very easily be targeting his next victims in San Diego. There were two murders left in the film, and that was what had Kevin so concerned.

"Do you know how we can contact Mr. Caine?" he asked.

Miles March began to flip through a Rolodex on his desk. "I have his cellular number right here; he is one of our biggest up-and-coming young stars; it's important that I am able to contact him at the drop of a hat." He plucked a card out of the Rolodex and handed it to Kevin, who in turn copied the number into his notebook.

"Can you think of anything else that may help our investigation?" he asked the movie maker as he and Carter rose to their feet.

March shook his head, and suddenly his face relaxed and a broad smile crept onto his face. "No, but this is beautiful… just perfect."

"What is?" Carter asked.

"I'm going to be making *Smash Hit 2*," he said. "It's going to go through the roof before it ever hits the box office. I guess I have Cory to thank for all of this, huh, gentlemen?"

Once again the two cops looked at each other with arched eyebrows, then thanked the man without shaking his hand. They let him know they would be in touch if they had any more questions, and that he should make himself readily available to them as needed. Finally, they left his office in silence. Before Kevin closed the door behind him he glanced at Miles March, who was watching them both leave, his grin still plastered to his face.

"That March is a weirdo," Carter said as they waited for the elevator. "All about the money in this industry, you know?"

"Yeah," Kevin replied as he cast a glance back toward the man's office door. "All about the money."

R.W.K. Clark

CHAPTER 15

Cory Caine was easy for Harmes and Carter to contact. All they had to do was dial his number, and the young man answered his phone on the second ring. It was obvious by the sound of his voice that he was enjoying all of the attention being afforded to him by the grisly murders and the success of his film.

The kid readily agreed to meet with them at one of the San Diego police substations. He was visiting one of his more recent girlfriends, and had no problem talking to the cops whatsoever. As a matter of fact, Harmes thought he sounded too eager.

San Diego was just under three hours away. Kevin and Carter got the go-ahead to fly, and hit the air for their two thirty appointment with the star of *Smash Hit*. As they flew, Kevin thought about the upcoming interview and the young movie star they were going to meet. Something just wasn't sitting well in his gut, but he couldn't identify or pin it down, and it was playing havoc on his ulcer.

Caine was already there when they arrived. When the two detectives approached the building he was standing outside entertaining the press, flashing big smiles, flirting mildly with the women, and turning on the overall charm. They stood in silence and watched the show for a short time before Kevin got sick of the syrupy crap and put an end to the press' heyday.

"Cory Caine?"

The kid turned to them and right away forgot about the press. "Are you the cops I'm going to be meeting with?"

Kevin nodded. "Yeah, but we won't be talking out here. Excuse me, folks, but Mr. Caine will be coming inside. You'll all have to finish this later, and I'm sure it won't be here at the station. Find another victim."

The press began to curse and mumble under their breath as they slowly dispersed. This was exactly the kind of thing that sucked about policing in Cali. Everything was a show, and everything was about publicity. It made it hard for a cop to do his best job.

He turned to Cory. "Let's go inside and talk."

Soon they were all seated in a small interview room with bottles of water. The chairs were cramped and the room was ice cold; Kevin was glad he wore a jacket, but the tanned movie star was in short sleeves, and the temperature didn't seem to be bothering him at all. He seemed calm, if not a bit excited that he was getting to talk to the cops.

"So," Kevin began. "You're here to visit your girl, huh?"

Cory shrugged. "She's not really my girl. I'm just getting to know her, you know what I mean?" He chuckled a bit and winked at Harmes. The kid acted like he didn't have a care in the world.

"How long are you going to be in town?" Kevin asked.

"Only a couple of days," he replied. "I head back to LA Sunday night, so I'm going to be partying it up while I'm here. Might as well put my free time to good use. But come Monday it's back to appearances and interviews."

"Does partying it up include murder?" Carter shot out.

Cory snapped his head in Carter's direction. "Murder? Wait, whoa, you're throwing me off, man! Are you thinking I'm the Box Office Butcher? Because you're nuts if you do."

To Kevin the kid looked genuinely surprised at the question, but he was an actor, after all. Probably like second nature for him to fake emotion. The two detectives watched him as he looked back and forth between them and waited for an answer.

"We hear you were in Sacramento last week," Kevin asked. "Is that so?"

Caine nodded vigorously. "Yeah, I was visiting my mother." He studied them both once again. "Is that why? Because I was in Sacramento when the murders happened?"

Now it was Kevin's turn to shrug. "It's a pretty good reason if you ask me."

"Well, I was in Sacramento." The kid stood up, the smile completely absent from his face. "Call my mom… she'll tell you. But I sure didn't kill anyone. I want to screw women, not murder them, guys."

Kevin watched him closely as he leaned his rear on a window sill and crossed his arms over his chest. "I'll get your mother's contact information. So, I also hear you acted a bit out of your league on the set."

"What do you mean?"

"Well, according to co-workers some of your behavior during the filming of *Smash Hit* wasn't what is required of an actor," Carter interjected. "Like trying to take care of jobs that aren't yours, maybe?"

Cory Caine's face scrunched up with genuine confusion. "I don't know what you're talking about. My job is to memorize my lines and be a certain character, and that's what I did. That's all I did. What do you mean?"

The detectives exchanged glances. The kid wasn't ever going to be an Oscar winner; Harmes knew that because he had seen *Smash Hit*. But he certainly was giving a convincing performance that day. He was starting to look freaked out, and he seemed to genuinely not know what the men were talking about.

"You didn't try to run the show?" Harmes asked. "Like, make things a little more believable?"

His confusion deepened. "No! I just do what March tells me. He'd flip if I tried to offer any advice to him, and I wouldn't want to. He's been in the biz a lot longer than me; I trust he knows what he's doing. I was made to be in front of the camera, not behind it."

Kevin decided right then and there he would request a tail from the San Diego PD, and he would ask them to keep on Caine for the rest of his stay. Something inside of him was telling him that this was a dead end, but one could never be sure. For now he would just get the kid's mom's information. Then he would pay her a visit.

Cory was allowed to leave after giving Harmes and Carter phone numbers and addresses where he could be reached, both in San Diego and back in LA. By the time he left, he was ready to run from the station house full speed ahead. He was jittery and nervous, and he skittered out of the place like a cockroach.

Harmes made arrangements for a temporary tail for the actor before he and Carter started out to visit with Cory's mom. The woman was in her forties, blond with her gray roots showing, and a cigarette dangling from the corner of her mouth. She seemed truly surprised that they were there.

Helena Caine was an abrasive woman, and she didn't take kindly to any of their questions, but Harmes didn't pick up on any dishonesty from her. She told them her son was with her during his entire visit, that he liked to see her now and again to escape the press' attention. Of course, her son wouldn't hurt a fly; he was a life-long lover, not a fighter.

∞

During the flight back to LA the two cops were able to discuss the day.

"What's your feeling on all of this, Harmes?" Carter asked him.

Kevin had his head back and his eyes closed. It looked as though he was patiently trying to rest, but the fact was his mind was racing. When he thought about Cory Caine and connected the kid to the murders in his mind, it just didn't taste right. Something was off.

"I'll be honest," he said to Carter. "I don't think it was him. Helena let us look around a bit, and there was nothing obvious in her home. No bloody clothes, nothing. Plus I don't think he's smart enough to have done it."

Carter grunted, obviously unconvinced. "I think we should get a warrant for his LA residence. The first two murders were here; maybe we'll find something there."

"Yep," Harmes replied simply; it was already on his list of things to do. He would take care of it as soon as they got back to LA.

For now he was going to catch a few winks and get a second wind.

∞

There were just two more acts to go, and the man had the players already picked out. Nothing was going to get in the way of him finishing his masterpiece. Not even the blithering cops.

Okay, so they were onto him. They knew it was somebody on the inside, someone close to *Smash Hit.* Yeah, it would have truly been hard for it to have been anyone else, now wouldn't it? But it didn't matter; he was too fast and too determined, and he was leaps and bounds ahead of them.

The Fifth Act (or should he say 'murder') in *Smash Hit* were going to be the most difficult out of the six to pull off. A young man and woman are both killed at the same time, while having sex. They were to be speared completely through both bodies at once, but that wasn't going to be the hard part. He was more than strong enough to do the job. The difficult part would be actually catching his intended victims while they were in the act.

He had chosen them carefully. Two junkies in San Diego who did nothing but take drugs and have sex. He had chosen them two months ago while doing business in town, and he had been monitoring them and their behavior together very carefully. They constantly did dope and then hit it together, screwing all over the place in the tiny, bug-infested apartment they called home. His concern wasn't that they wouldn't have sex, but that they might go to jail or break up before he carried out the Act. So, as a type of insurance, he had been sending cash, once a week, in the mail, anonymously. No need to engage in crime; he saw to it they stayed high.

The sixth victim was going to be a little old man who lived in a small cottage. He was deaf, just like the last victim in the film, and he would be the easiest to victimize. He would need to gut the old man and leave his intestines on the floor next to the body, but that was nothing.

In *Smash Hit*, the killer was taken down by cops right after the final murder. He is found with the old man's tongue in a baggie in his jacket pocket, and it turned out that the killer targeted the man because he had raped his mother, which resulted in the birth of the killer in the film. He took his tongue because that was what had been done to the mother after her rape.

The old man who would be the last victim was the easiest to find, because he was the point of the entire masterpiece.

He couldn't wait to get his hands on the so-and-so's tongue.

CHAPTER 16

Harmes and Carter sat in Harmes' office at the precinct and discussed the findings from the execution of the search warrant on Cory Caine's high-rise penthouse, and it wasn't a very in-depth conversation at all.

The fact of the matter was that the young actor's apartment had been totally clean. There weren't even any weapons with a trace of blood or tissue on them. No bloody clothing, no blood in the drains. His car, which was in the underground garage, was also processed, and once again, there was nothing.

"I just don't think it's him," Harmes said to Carter as he stared inside his styrofoam coffee cup and stirred at the beverage with his swizzle stick.

Carter shook his head. "How do we account for location? How do we account for the fact that he has been everywhere the murders happened when they happened? I'm just not convinced he is as dumb or incapable as he would have us think he is."

"I have another idea, Joe," Kevin said.

Joe Carter stared at him, waiting, then finally said, "Well?"

"I think we need to check out Miles March."

Joe knit his brow. "The director? Oh, heck no. This guy has more to lose than anyone. He's raking in the dough, and he is going to make number two. I don't know, Kev. Seems off."

"Yeah, he's raking it in, all right," Kevin replied. "But consider these points: the murders are what happen to be 'raking in the dough'. He is an alpha male from the get-go; just look at how he acted and talked, even to us. He is completely confident. And even Cory Caine said he takes directions from the director, not the other way around."

"So, what do you want to do?"

Kevin shrugged and sat back. "I want to interview him again."

∞

The telephone in Kevin's office was on speaker, and he and Carter were listening to it ring as they waited for Miles March to answer. He was out of town, and had left on his flight the same evening they had met with him at Milestone Pictures. According to his secretary, he was in Santa Clara, meeting with investors regarding the second installment of *Smash Hit*. When Harmes found out that March had a private jet and that he couldn't just verify where the flight landed, he called the man's cell himself.

At first it went to voicemail, but neither Harmes nor Carter left a message. Kevin just simply hung up and redialed the cell number. He did this four times, with the speaker on, before Miles March finally answered. When he did answer, he sounded pissed.

"What is your problem?" he greeted them rudely.

Harmes and Carter held each other's eyes. "Mr. March, this is Detective Harmes from the LAPD. We spoke last week?"

The man was silent for a moment. "I'm sorry, Detective. I'm in a meeting right now, and your calls have managed to cause quite a bit of stress."

"Where are you, Mr. March?" Kevin asked.

The man cleared his throat. "I'm in Santa Clara. What does that have to do with anything?"

Now it was Carter's turn. "When will you be returning? We need to meet with you to verify some of the information you gave us."

"Not until Monday, perhaps Tuesday," he said in a short voice. "Detectives, I am a very busy man. You don't get where I am by sitting on your bum and calling people from the comfort of a desk. I travel, and I travel often, for the films I make."

Carter rolled his eyes and Kevin smiled. "So, when will you be back in LA?"

"Oh, late Monday or early Tuesday, depending on how things go here, if I can ever get back to it."

"I'll get a hold of you then, Mr. March," Kevin said pleasantly. "Thanks for your time."

He quickly punched the disconnect button before March could respond, then he looked at Carter. "Let's head to the airport. I think it's time to see Mr. Miles March's flight logs."

∞

"Let's see, two weeks ago I have Mr. March in Aspen for the weekend. Last weekend he was Vegas, and this weekend it looks to me he will be in Santa Clara till Monday."

Carter stood by tapping his foot impatiently. Kevin knew his colleague thought March was nothing more than an innocent egotist, and he might very well have been right. But Kevin Harmes was all about ruling suspects out, and that was what he would do with March. Besides, it couldn't hurt.

He had the young lady at the airport make copies of the logs for his records, then the two detectives started back for the precinct. "I told you it wasn't going to be March, Kevin. The guy has been making films for years; he isn't going to risk his fame or his standing in the industry, you know?"

Kevin nodded, but he didn't speak. Maybe Carter was right and he was barking up the wrong tree. It was Friday, and the investigation had been taking a lot out of him.

"Okay, okay," he said. "How about this: we both go home, eat, and get some sleep. The weekend is here, and if there are going to be more murders we won't know until they happen. If they do we can see where they happen. That should help us, hopefully, to narrow things down even more."

So, he dropped his partner off at the station, switched cars, and made his way home. Harmes put the television news on, microwaved a TV dinner, and grabbed a half-bottle of whisky and a dusty glass. It would be nice to fall asleep on his own couch for once.

The news was the same old: local crimes, weather and sports, and one announcement pleading with people to 'be careful' because the Box Office Butcher hadn't finished killing, according to the movie. Harmes was sick over it; everyone was acting like the murders were a big joke, a publicity stunt of some kind. No one was safe.

A late-night talk show came on, but by then Kevin was already dozing off. He was four double-shots deep, and his ability to stay awake was gone entirely. His last thought was that tomorrow was a new day.

∞

It was ten fifteen at night in San Diego. The man stood in the closet silently, his eyes peering through the slatted door, focused hard on the two people sitting on the grimy mattress on the floor. He held a strong spear in his hand, and the spear was even taller than he was. He was excited to get to use it.

Little Mister and Miss Junkie had returned to the apartment from scoring some meth after finding an extra-fat envelope in their mailbox. Yay! An unexpected treat. Now they were sitting on the mattress jabbing themselves with needles while some heavy metal garbage played on the clock radio next to them.

It was only a matter of time now.

He watched as the guy took the needle out of his arm and tossed it into a box. He stood and pushed a tape into an ancient VCR that was situated on top of an old tube television. He pressed play and the sounds of slutty sex began pouring from the television's speaker along with cheesy music. True to form, they were putting in porn.

The guy's hand went directly to his crotch and he got comfortable on the mattress while Little Miss finished her blast. His eyes were anxiously going from the TV to the girl, but he didn't have to wait long; she was almost done, and soon she stood and began dancing and shaking her rear in front of him.

For a killer he was certainly patient. He had been in the closet waiting for this for the last few hours. Now, both of them were getting naked. They were slathering each other with kisses and groping each other from top to bottom. The guy kept one eye faithfully on the porn even as he mounted her and began humping away.

He didn't wait another second. He stepped from the closet, took two long strides, held the spear over his head, and brought it down. Just before it impaled the twisted lovers the guy glanced at him and opened his mouth to scream, but he never had a chance. The killer pinned them to the floor through the mattress. Both of their eyes were wide open, and blood was pouring from their mouths as they twitched incessantly.

He stood and watched, the male gave one last jerk, and as their breath left both of their bodies he groaned and smiled.

Even the perfect music had been playing for The Fifth Act; thank goodness for porn.

R.W.K. Clark

CHAPTER 17

Kevin Harmes was dreaming.

He was in a house, but he wasn't alone. A young girl of about twenty-three was walking around dusting and straightening. She was watching a movie on a huge movie screen that filled up an entire wall, or maybe the wall was the screen. Kevin could hear screams, and he looked to the screen to see the movie *Smash Hit* playing. It was on one of the murder scenes, though in his dream he couldn't make out which one.

He could clearly see the girl who lived in the house. She was tiny, no more than five feet tall. She was cleaning and turning to the screen to watch while she did her work. She couldn't see Kevin, and he knew it. He began to approach her from behind, because he knew that she was going to be the next victim, and he wanted to warn her. The closer he got to her, though, the further away from him she would get.

Suddenly, a knock came to the front door of the house. The sounds from the movie stopped, and the girl turned to the door, a bit surprised. She smiled at it, as though she had been expecting someone.

"Who is it?" she called out in a sing-song voice.

But no one answered, and Kevin knew it was the Box Office Butcher. He tried to grab her arm so he could turn her around to look her in the face. He wanted to stop her and tell her: No! Don't open it! But no matter how many times he tried to grab her arm, his hand simply went through it as though she were made of smoke.

The knock came again, more persistent this time.

"I'm coming!" she sang out again, and she made her way to the door. When she got to it she stopped and called out once again, "Who is it?"

"No!" Kevin screamed, but no sound came out. The knocking got harder and louder, but she was frozen there, not moving. It came in sharp consecutive raps, which seemed to get louder each and every time.

Suddenly, she turned to him, and in a low voice that Kevin could just hear through the knocking, said, "It's only just beginning, you know."

She reached out to open the door. The knocks were so hard now that the entire house was shaking. He opened his mouth once more to scream at her, to beg her to stop, leave the door locked and closed, but she turned the knob and...

He sat up straight on his own couch in his own small house. The glass he had been drinking whisky out of fell from beside him and hit the floor with a loud thunk. It was then that he heard the knocking on his own door. Kevin shook his head and struggled to get his wits about him.

"Who is it?" he yelled.

There was a pause. "It's Carter, Harmes. Open up. Rise and shine."

Kevin staggered across the room and opened the door to see Detective Joe Carter standing there with a serious look on his face.

"Did you get enough sleep, Kev?" he asked.

Kevin stifled a yawn and squinted through the sunlight that was hitting him dead in the face. "Is there such a thing?"

"I hope," Carter replied. "There has been another Butcher killing, a couple of junkies."

Now he was wide awake. "Where?"

"San Diego."

∞

The ride to the precinct was used primarily for filling Kevin Harmes in on exactly what Carter had learned. They had been trying to get him on his cell for three hours, but the out-of-date device had been dead, and Joe had had come to drag him back to reality.

"This is what we know: two druggies, both twenty-five. Marissa Gooden and Mick Newman. The pair have been together for a few years." Joe was driving the car while Kevin sipped coffee desperately.

"How do we know it's the Butcher?" Kevin asked.

Joe looked at him. "You should know: just like the fifth murders in the movie. A couple having sex, speared clean through. Pinned to the floor and dead, they were."

"Who found them?"

Carter put his eyes back on the road. "The girl's sister. She went to their place to take Miss Gooden to her house to do laundry. When they didn't answer she used her key to get in. According to the sister they were both meth-heads. She had a key just in case something like an OD happened."

"We need to head to San Diego," Kevin said. "We need to bring in Cory Caine."

Carter chuckled. "You're on top of nothing for an old sleepyhead. They already have him. We have to stop at the station for our files and go down and interview him ourselves."

"What about the tail we had on him?" Kevin asked. "Did they witness him leaving home or anything?"

"Don't know any more right now," Carter replied. "We'll be learning together."

They flew to San Diego, flying like a bird of prey on a mission. Very little was said between the two; Kevin reviewed the files and spoke when he wanted to run something by Carter about the case. But Carter didn't have much to say; he knew that Harmes was already lining things up in his mind.

They arrived at the SDPD, where they were escorted to the same interview room as before. This time would be different, Harmes knew. This time they would have a video camera on the other side of the two-way mirror, taping everything they said and did. He was fine with that. If Caine was the killer he would be nabbed today. If he wasn't Harmes would soon find out.

He was brought in by a uniformed officer, and he was a mess. Cory Caine's eyes were red-rimmed and puffy; he had obviously been crying. He was both cuffed and shackled. No one was taking any chances.

He sat in a chair across the table from Harmes and Carter. "I can't believe this is happening," he croaked. "I didn't do this thing, you guys. You've got to believe me."

Harmes smirked. "Where were you last night?"

"With Mindy Cooper, the girl I've been seeing," he said. "Right where I told you I'd be, and I never left, not once."

According to the tail they had put on Caine, this was true. Officers stated that they never observed him leaving the residence at all. Not only that, when they arrested him they searched both his girlfriend's place and her car, and they found nothing in either one.

"So, how did you get out?" Carter pressed.

Caine looked at him as if he had lost his mind. "I told you, I never left! We got drunk and smoked a little grass, but all we did was have sex and pass out, I swear!"

Mindy Cooper was being interviewed down the hall, and Kevin knew she was saying the same thing.

"So, tell me, Cory," Kevin began, "Is that why you tried to pressure Miles March into letting you ad lib murder scenes? Is it because you wanted to practice these murders ahead of time? Because that's how it looks to me."

Now Caine's face froze. He stared at Harmes for a long moment, then got an unidentifiable look in his eyes. "Is that what you meant at the first interview? When you asked if I tried to get things done my way?"

Kevin nodded, a false smug look on his face as he tried to bluff. "Yep. Is that it, Cory? Was the movie 'rehearsal'?"

Now the kid looked pissed. His eyes narrowed, and he said in a low voice, "Who told you that?"

"Your boss, Miles March."

Cory sat back in his chair and shook his head. "I don't know why he would tell you that, but it's a lie. Ask the rest of the cast. Ask the crew. March runs things all the way. We did 'ad lib' the murders when we taped, but he said it was to get a genuine, unrehearsed reaction from the 'victims'. It was never my idea."

Kevin looked over at Carter to see the man already looking at him. They both were thinking the same thing, and the arched eyebrows proved it. Cory Caine had nothing to do with these murders. He was just an actor in a horror movie.

Harmes jumped up. "Okay, if that's your story, I guess we're through here. We have no evidence, and even your tail didn't see you leave. We need to do some checking, but hopefully you won't be here long."

The detectives left the room without another word, leaving Cory to ask questions as they left that they wouldn't answer. They stepped into the observation room on the other side of the two-way mirror, and Kevin was the first to speak. He wanted to make sure this innocent kid didn't suffer any more.

"He didn't do this," he told the San Diego detective clearly. "But I'm pretty sure I know who did."

∞

An hour later Cory Caine left through the back sally port of the holding area. He was dressed and ready to leave the stinking place. After those LA cops had left, he had been released almost immediately. He figured they would keep him in their radar; that's what they did on TV and in the movies anyway. But he didn't care, because he hadn't done anything wrong.

Mindy Cooper drove, and they were able to sneak out of the lot easily and avoid the press, thanks to the cops letting them leave out the back exit. Cory was far from finished with the situation, though. He was going right back to Mindy's place and he was going to make a phone call to Miles March. He didn't know what that demanding so-and-so had in mind when he led the cops to him, but Cory was going to call him on it right away.

Mindy made him a drink while he made the call, which March picked up after two rings.

"Miles March."

Cory wanted to punch him in his throat, but he kept calm. "Mr. March, it's Cory Caine."

There was a brief pause. "Cory! I hear you were in a… bit of trouble. Is there anything I can do to help? Hire a good lawyer for you maybe?"

"I don't need a lawyer, March. I'm out. They didn't charge me; they made some kind of mistake." He could feel his skin crawl with anger. March offered to get him an attorney when he lied to the cops about him? "The cops said you told them some things about my behavior on the set that weren't true."

"Things?" the man asked. "I don't know…"

Cory growled into the phone. "Listen, Miles. I think we should talk when I get back to LA. Some of the things they said, well, helped make sense out of a lot of your little habits on set, if you know what I mean."

Miles March didn't hesitate. "No need to wait. Are you still in San Diego?"

"Yeah," Caine replied. "Just got out of jail. Shitty way to spend a Saturday, and it all comes back to you."

March cleared his throat. "How about if I jet to you and meet you. I never meant any harm, and this is nothing more than a misunderstanding, I'm sure. We can definitely talk about it. Where are you? We can clear this up easily enough. I'll even call the police and talk to them if you wish, Cory."

Caine thought about it for a minute. This might be the best way to be a shoe-in on March's next picture. There had been plenty of rumors about a *Smash Hit 2* around the studio, and maybe he could be written in, even though his character was polished off in the first. They did it all the time in horror films.

"Was this just some kind of publicity stunt, Miles?" he asked, his voice like that of an unsure child.

March just chuckled. "Sort of. You'd be surprised what publicity can do for a career, Cory. What's the address where you are? We'll talk, and I'll fill you in on everything."

∞

Miles March hung up his cell and sat back. Yes, things were coming to a bit of a head now, and the timing couldn't have been more perfect. This was going to pan out far better than he ever could have hoped or dreamed. His masterpiece was almost complete, and no one would stop him.

He stood and shut off the DVD of *Smash Hit* he had playing on the television. He had been going over the final murder scene time and time again, just as he had with all the rest. He wasn't right where he needed to be, but Cory Caine had managed to interrupt him. He was surprised; he'd truly thought Cory would be locked up for a bit. No matter, though; he could string this out a bit longer, long enough to finish the masterpiece.

He let his robe drop to the floor and began changing clothes. When he was finished he fished through one of his bags and withdrew a buckled leather pouch. From it, he removed one of the filet knives with the pronged end; it was his favorite, after all. He loved to get up close and personal. The spear was boring, but the public loved variety when it came to murder; one had to get creative.

Next, March put his hat on his head and dialed a local cab company. He arranged for a taxi to meet him a block away at a bar to take him to the place Cory was. He would have the cab drop him a block from there as well, and then he would creep around until he could get in unseen. It wouldn't be too hard; he would call Cory and have him meet him, then escort him up. Sometimes you had to do things the hard way and suffer for your art. It would be a busy night: taking care of Cory, then finishing the Final Act.

But most of all it was because Cory's girlfriend, Mindy Cooper, would have to die too. A triple play, all in one day. He just couldn't help but smile.

CHAPTER 18

Kevin Harmes and Joe Carter stood in the San Diego apartment home of Mindy Cooper in silence. The place was milling with cops and crime scene investigators, all of them either standing over the dead young woman's mangled body or conducting some other kind of investigative techniques. Kevin was really paying them all no mind though; he was too busy being furious.

Of course, Cory Caine couldn't be found, which made the kid look all the more guilty, but Kevin wasn't buying into it. He was stuck on Miles March in his mind, but the situation certainly looked grim for Caine, at least on initial observation. It appeared the kid had panicked, killed off his girlfriend, and run for the hills. Upon getting the call from the San Diego PD, that was how it sounded.

But then the old man was found across San Diego from the Cooper girl's murder. Myron Dennis, a 68-year-old who had been convicted for rape some twenty years before, was found mutilated and hanging from a beam that went across the living room ceiling in his small cottage home by his mailman, who claimed to have a package for the old man to sign. The old man was always home, and when he didn't answer the door the mailman looked through the front window and saw him dangling.

A background check on the old man brought up the old rape charge, and it also revealed to Kevin that the man had been suspected of several other rapes but never convicted. It really wasn't that information that bothered Harmes, though. It was the fact that the old man was found with his own tongue in his hand, and that was how the final victim was found in *Smash Hit*. It looked like the perp had made his way through every murder in the film at last. Whether the killer was the missing Cory Caine, producer and director Miles March, or someone else entirely, he had gotten the job done.

That pissed Kevin Harmes off to no end.

He turned to Joe Carter and elbowed the man in the arm. "Let's get out of here. The local PD has an all-points bulletin out on Caine; I want to call Miles March and see if he has heard from his star at all. But I also want to see how he responds to the news that the kid's girlfriend is dead and he is missing. His reaction might tell us something."

As they left the apartment Harmes tried the cell number of March, who was supposed to be in Santa Clara, according to his flight logs. The phone rang several times before finally going to voice mail. Kevin didn't leave a message; he just hung up the phone and grunted.

"I guess we'll have to try again later," he told Carter. "But I gotta tell you, man. I have a bad feeling about this. They aren't going to find Cory alive. Mark my words."

∞

The closet was pitch black and freezing cold.

Little Donny was crouched on the floor in the darkness, his arms wrapped around his knees and his mouth pressed against them to keep him from making a sound. Outside of the closet things were crashing into walls and against the closet door. He could hear the gurgling of his furious mother as she had her temper tantrum, the second one so far that day.

It was barely lunchtime.

But Donny was used to it. Ever since he'd been born, he'd had to withstand her hatred toward him and her blows. He was just seven, but his young age didn't stop her, and it hadn't stopped her from telling him just why she hated him two years ago. She couldn't speak, but she had drawn him pictures, and they were clear.

Whoever his daddy was, he was the reason Donny's mommy hated him. Donny didn't understand the reason entirely. He just knew that his daddy had hurt his mommy, and that was how she got Donny. She also told him that his daddy had been the one who had taken her tongue; he had done it to keep her from telling on him.

Donny's mommy used to be in movies. Two of them; Donny had watched them for himself. She had been pretty when she was young, and she'd also had a very pretty voice. Now all she did was groan and gurgle and screech, just like she was doing now. Donny moved his hands and put them tightly over his ears as something glass shattered against the closet door.

Someday Donny would find his daddy; he made a promise to himself that he would. He would ask his daddy why he hurt his mommy so bad, why he made it to where she couldn't talk in words. Then maybe, just maybe, Donny would steal his daddy's tongue so his daddy would know how it felt.

But for now he was just seven, and his mommy was mad at him again. The closet door flew open and without missing a beat Donny skittered across the floor and around his mother's legs. A loud screech came out of her mouth as she spun and tried to grab at his ankles, but he slipped from her grasp and she lost her balance and tumbled to the floor. Donny quickly crawled into the nearest corner and stared back at her in horror as she tried to pick herself up. He knew he was in real trouble then; he had made mommy fall.

She ran to him and grabbed him by his hair and began to drag him across the floor. He tried to kick and squirm to get away from her, but she had a firm grasp on his head. He didn't dare speak or yell, because one of the reasons she hated him was because he could talk and she couldn't. He was going to have to stop fighting and let her punish him, or he would make it much worse than it had to be.

She pulled him into the kitchen and sat on his chest, holding his arms down with her knees. Her lips were moving with incalculable speed, but no sounds came out, of course. It didn't matter; Donny knew what she was saying: he was filthy and ugly and just like his father; all he did was cause her pain. Since he learned to read well she had written this in notes countless times.

She reached up and grabbed the knife from the counter, the one with two points on the top of the blade. With it she cut his red and white striped t-shirt from his body, and Donny began to cry in earnest. She looked down at him and smiled as she waved the knife before his eyes.

"No, Mommy, please," he whimpered. "I'll be a good boy now. I promise."

But just as though she hadn't heard him she raked the blade across his skin. It stung him, and more tears poured out of his eyes. But Donny bit the inside of his lips and stayed quiet. If he made another sound it wouldn't end for hours.

After she cut him seven times, one for each year he had been alive, his mommy looked at his face for the first time since the cutting began. He had passed out from the pain. No more tears, no more words, and no more sounds, just as it should be.

Miles March was pulled violently from the dream by the chirping of his cellular phone. He picked it up and squinted at the number: it was that cop again. They must have found that whiny little broad Mindy Cooper's body. He smiled to himself; they were looking for Cory Caine, and he knew it. Perfect.

He answered the phone, his smile still intact. "Miles March."

"Mr. March, this is Detective Harmes," the voice answered. "Hope I didn't disturb you, but the Box Office Butcher case has taken a turn. Are you still in Santa Clara?"

Miles stood and flipped on the lamp on the nightstand. The bedside clock read eleven-thirty in the morning. It was Sunday, and he had finished the Final Act of his masterpiece. He walked to the heavy black drapes to open them and let the sunlight in.

"No, Detective," he replied. "As a matter of fact, I'm not. I flew back to LA last night. How can I help you?"

Harmes cleared his throat. "Have you spoken to Cory Caine, by chance?"

March's smile grew. "No. No, I haven't. Is something wrong?"

It may have been Kevin Harmes' imagination, but he could swear that March's voice sounded… pleased. "We have his girlfriend dead, another *Smash Hit* murder, and a missing male lead, who just happened to be a suspect. So, I guess I was hoping you had seen or heard from Mr. Caine."

March was silent for, what seemed to Kevin, to be an extended amount of time. He couldn't even hear the man's breath. Finally, he was compelled to ask, "Are you still there, Mr. March?"

"Yes, yes," came the reply. "I'm here. Listen, I'll be going into the office soon. If my secretary has heard from Cory I'll be the first to know. I'll call you right away. I will be leaving for a pre-casting vacation before the filming of *Smash Hit 2* this week, so I will be sure to keep my eyes and ears peeled in the meantime. How does that sound?"

Was it Kevin's imagination, or did he seem to be racing, as if trying to think and offer responses that would temporarily appease? He took a deep breath and said, "That would be fine. I'll look forward to hearing from you soon."

When the call was terminated, March let his mind wander back to the dream. It sparked a heavy feeling in his stomach, and anger began to well up inside of him. He let himself focus on the emotion for a moment before standing and putting on a satin robe. Then he made his way downstairs to the door of the basement. As he turned the knob and trotted down the steps he began to hum to himself.

A large deep-freeze unit was in a small area to the left at the bottom of the steps. A combination lock dangled from the door, and Miles March continued to hum as he spun the dial back and forth expertly. In less than a minute he popped it and opened the freezer door.

Cory Caine was tucked neatly inside of the freezer. He was wrapped in heavy plastic, and duct tape was wound securely around his body in three different areas. He was safe and sound, and even though Detective Harmes' call had startled him because he hadn't been all the way awake, he was able to now breathe a sigh of relief.

"Yes, Detective Harmes," he muttered through a sarcastic grin, "I have seen Cory Caine. I made it a point to let him know you are looking for him."

March let the freezer door slam shut, then secured the padlock once again before letting his hum turn to a whistle. Time to shower and begin to plan his next step. In his mind, that meant heading to the studio to make an appearance; he had another movie to begin production on, and he could hardly wait.

He showered and dressed, then fished a large shoe box out of a safe he kept in the back of his bedroom closet. He opened it and began to shuffle through the photos and newspaper articles inside. They were all about the mother of a boy named Donovan Cannon. She was an actress who had been raped and mutilated, and wound up pregnant by her attacker. The rapist had cut her tongue out in an effort that was supposed to ensure she would never talk or identify him.

Miles March was Donovan Cannon; his mother had been Ruth Cannon, a 'scream queen' in the late sixties. She had hated him to the point of abuse, and all Donovan had ever tried to do was earn her love. Well, his masterpiece had been his coup de grâce, his final homage to her suffering, and his final attempt at earning, from a dead woman, the love he had never received.

Yes, he thought as he returned the items to the box, she is finally happy with Donny now.

He had a plan, a plan that would ensure he would be able to remain free and functional. But for now, it was important that he save face and get to the studio. After all, the cops were obviously buying his Cory Caine smoke and mirrors act.

Cory was going to be more valuable in death than he ever had been in life.

R.W.K. Clark

CHAPTER 19

Kevin Harmes hung up the phone after speaking with Miles March and looked across his desk at Joe Carter.

"Well?" Carter prompted. "Has he seen or heard from Caine?"

Harmes leaned forward, shrugged, and took a sip from the cold coffee in the small, styrofoam cup on his desk. "He says he hasn't. If Caine is the killer, and he is on the lam, I don't expect him to show up to work today anyway. But I've gotta tell you, Joe, I'm not so sure."

Carter gave him a crazy look. "What do you mean, Kev? His girl, Mindy Cooper, is found dead in the middle of a bloodbath. Caine, who we knew was with her, is nowhere to be found. The murders in the movie are wrapped up, so who else could it be? Maybe Miss Cooper discovered something and Caine was forced to take her out. That's my theory."

"And it would seem like a good one," Kevin replied. "But that's just it: the movie murders are complete. The perp was just about as exacting as he could be, without being able to predict the reactions and responses of his victims. Mindy Cooper shouldn't have died. The murders are supposedly over."

"So, what's next?"

Kevin sat back and thought about it. He would wait to hear from March, and in the meantime he and Carter would fly to Sacramento to speak with Cory Caine's mother, who had told police she hadn't seen him or heard from him. Maybe there was something everyone else was missing.

"Let's have a talk with Momma," Kevin finally said. "If she does know where the kid is, maybe we can get it out of her with a little patience and TLC."

As they left the station house Kevin couldn't help but pay attention to the nagging feeling he felt inside. Something just wasn't right, but once again he couldn't put a finger on it. For now he would have to bide his time, at least until things cleared up better in his head.

∞

Miles March hadn't told the truth about being in LA.

Oh, he fully planned to be there for a mid-morning meeting, but when he talked to Harmes he had actually still been in San Diego. No need to offer up any extra information, though. After all, that would be like doing the cops' work for them.

He had left his place after looking through his shoebox with every intention of flying back to LA for the meeting, but he had changed his mind. He was beginning to feel a bit nervous, so he called the others who were going to attend the meeting and rescheduled for the following day. Things felt a bit loose around the edges, as though they were a bit out of control. It made the metallic taste of panic fill his mouth, but he didn't know why.

So, he had let his secretary know, after asking if she had seen Cory Caine, that he had some other business to take care of there in the city, but he decided to stay in San Diego for one more night to do some thinking. He needed to smooth things out and regain whatever control he thought he had lost. So, now he was back in his home in San Diego, sitting on the toilet in the master bathroom, dragging a razor across the skin of his upper thigh. As the blood dripped to the floor he felt the anxiety leave right along with it.

He wasn't going to get caught. He had planned too long and too hard to let things fall apart now. He was intelligent, accomplished, and rich, and nothing was going to stop this personal masterpiece from serving its purpose.

After a half-hour he cleaned himself and the bathroom, then put on clean clothes. At second thought he might take his mini-vacation at one of his other homes in LA, far from San Diego. He would relax and revel in the success of *Smash Hit*, and in the success of the revenge he had taken on behalf of his mother.

He had earned it.

Sacramento was a bust.

Cory Caine's mother was so grief-stricken over the disappearance of her son that she wouldn't even let Harmes and Carter into her home. They spoke to other officers on the case locally, and all of them were of the same opinion: Cory Caine was the Box Office Butcher. To the mother it was a missing person case; to the cops it was the hunt for a killer.

By the time they arrived back in LA it was nearly six in the evening, but Harmes wasn't ready to throw in the towel for the day. He pointed the car in the direction of Milestone Pictures and continued to drive in silence. Carter immediately began to get edgy.

"What are we doing?"

Harmes shrugged. "I thought we would just stop by Milestone. With a new picture in the works I'm guessing that March will be at the studio. I'm just wondering if he heard from Caine."

"He would have called you," Carter stated in a perturbed voice. "But it's Sunday. Don't you believe in sleep?"

Kevin ignored the man. "It will give us a chance to interview some of the other cast and crew that are hanging out. You know these people work late into the night. I just wanna give it a shot, okay?"

The two men parked and flashed their badges, and soon they were riding the elevator to the top floor where Miles March's office was. "We'll start there first, then mingle and ask some more questions. I'll bet March isn't in anyway."

They got off the elevator and entered the lobby area, which was dark and dim from the lights being lowered for the evening. It seemed deserted at first, but then Kevin took notice of March's secretary standing in the shadows behind her desk. She was putting a sweater on, and stopped dead in her tracks when she saw the two detectives.

"Can I help you?" she asked in an unsure voice. "The studio is closed."

Kevin flashed her a smile in the darkness, which prompted her to flip a switch; light then flooded the lobby.

"Hi. Good to see you again," Kevin began. "Just working the case. I spoke to Mr. March this morning and he told me he would be coming in for a meeting and he would let me know if anything had been heard from Cory Caine. I take it March is gone for the evening?"

The woman looked a bit confused. "When did you talk to him? Because Mr. March didn't come in today. The meeting was postponed. He did ask me to let him know if Cory came in, but he hasn't."

Kevin glanced at Carter before continuing. "He missed the meeting? I figured it was too important to miss, especially since he flew back to LA especially for it."

She shot another confused look. "I didn't think he had returned yet. Listen, I really have to go; can I leave him a message that you stopped by?"

Kevin studied her briefly. "No. It's not a big deal. I'll be in touch with him tomorrow, then. Have a good night."

They began making their way back to the car. Kevin was silent, and Carter noticed it. Kevin did not speak a word since they left the lobby area; he was walking with energy and purpose, and Carter was having a difficult time keeping up.

"What's up, man?" he asked as they climbed into the car.

As Kevin started the engine he replied, "Something's not right." He began to drive full of intent and purpose, and Carter picked up on it all right away.

"So, where are we going?"

Harmes kept his vision straight ahead. He cleared his throat and said, "Back to LAX. Time to pay a return visit to the private strips. If Miles March lied to me about being in LA, then where has he been?"

CHAPTER 20

"Let's see… I show a flight coming in to LA yesterday evening."

The young man was standing with a clipboard in his hand, staring down at the sheet on top of it and scanning it with his eyes. His brow was knit as he concentrated. After a moment he nodded and looked up at Kevin.

"Yep. Yesterday evening."

Kevin looked at his partner. "So, I guess March was telling the truth; he did come back to LA."

The kid interjected. "Yeah, I mean, it's possible. Like I said, the flight log records state that March-Air 3 arrived here at eight-thirty-three last evening. But that doesn't mean Mr. March was on it."

Kevin swung his head back to the young man. "What do you mean? Why would the plane land and Mr. March not be on it?"

The kid with the badge that read 'Travis Cole' gave the two officers a chuckle. "Well, he could have been, but with Mr. March there really is no telling. After all, the man has three planes; he could have been on any one of them."

Carter and Harmes spoke in unison. "Three planes? How did we miss this before?"

Travis offered them a nod. "I'm not sure. I only work weekends." Then began to walk back toward the front counter where they had found him. He tossed the clipboard down and began tapping on the computer which sat before him. He had told them he had a lot of work to do when they first arrived.

"Yes. Three planes," he replied. "Mr. March has quite a few business-related ventures which require the use of his jets; he isn't always a passenger. Now, if you'll excuse me."

The kid began to type in earnest, prompting Kevin to reach over the top of the counter and slam his hand down on the keyboard. Travis Cole's head jerked up in surprise.

"What the heck?"

Kevin smirked. "Listen... Mr. Cole, is it? I want to know all about these planes. I want to know where each and every one flew to and from for the last three weekends. And I want it now."

He removed his hand and straightened up. Travis stared at him for a minute, then obviously resigned himself to the fact that he was going to have to spend more time not getting his own work done. He looked back down at the computer screen and began tapping lightly on the keyboard.

"Okay, fine," he began. "It will take me a moment to pull up the information. We have March-Air 1, 2, and 3. You said three consecutive weeks back from today, correct?"

"Correct," both Carter and Harmes said in unison.

After about three minutes the young man looked up. "Okay." The detectives nodded in response.

Harmes spoke up. "Look under the fourth and fifth of this month first."

Travis looked back down at the screen. "On the fourth, March-Air 1 made a flight to Sydney, New South Wales. It didn't return until Sunday. March-Air 2 left on the afternoon of the fourth for New York City, and it returned early Sunday morning. March-Air 3 was grounded all weekend for maintenance."

"Was Mr. March on either of the two flights that left?" Carter asked.

Travis shook his head impatiently. "I only work weekends, remember, and it isn't specific on either of the flights whether or not Mr. March was a passenger."

"So move on to the flights on the eleventh through the thirteenth," Kevin demanded. "That was the weekend of the Sacramento killings."

Travis did a bit more tapping. "Okay. The morning of Friday the eleventh, two flights left. One went to Austin, Texas and returned Saturday night just before midnight; the other went to Sacramento and didn't return until Sunday afternoon. March-Air 1 was grounded for maintenance, and no, it doesn't say which, if either, flight Mr. March was on."

Finally, Kevin requested the flights for the eighteenth through the twentieth, the weekend which had just passed, the weekend of the San Diego killings.

"Number three went to Butte, Montana early Friday afternoon and returned here, to LA, at eight thirty-three Saturday evening, just like I said, and just like Mr. March told you," Travis said stiffly. "Number one went to San Diego, and it has not yet returned, but it looks like it is due back first thing tomorrow morning."

Harmes looked at Carter and both of them raised their eyebrows. "Tell me, Travis," Harmes continued. "Do you know if Mr. March has a hotel chain preference when he travels out of town?" It seemed to Kevin that the only way they were going to be able to place the man in one town or another was through hotel records.

Travis Cole shook his head. "All I can tell you is that Mr. March won't stay in a hotel at all if he can help it; he has homes all over the country. Rumor has it that he has several out of the country as well. A lot of the guys make cracks about it, you know? About how nice it must be to be such a rich so-and-so. And the guy acts…"

He looked up from the computer but the two cops were gone. He glanced around the room for a minute before shrugging and turning back to his own work.

Travis didn't give the two detectives, or their questions, another thought.

∞

"I'm telling you, Joe, something is going on with Miles March."

It was getting very late, and while Joe Carter was tired and hungry, Kevin Harmes seemed to be just waking up. He was sitting forward in the driver's seat, directing the car along the freeway with purpose and direction. Joe wanted to keep up, but he was on the verge of exhaustion.

"Can't it wait 'til morning?" he asked Kevin. "March would be back then, if he is on the San Diego plane."

Kevin took the off ramp and turned toward the station house. "I'll tell you what: you go home, eat, and get some sleep. I'm going to find out about these homes; I want to know where all of them are exactly. I'll catch a few z's during the night, but I'm going to get on the computer and learn a little bit more about Mr. Miles March. In the morning, when you come back, we'll pay a little visit to him at Milestone Pictures."

So, it was settled. Joe Carter jumped in his personal vehicle and left, while Kevin Harmes went to his office with a steaming cup of station house coffee and his file on the Box Office Butcher. His focus was no longer on Cory Caine at all; in fact, he was convinced in his mind that Cory Caine was dead somewhere. Kevin was at the point where he was on the verge of being convinced that the famous producer and director Miles March had been blowing smoke up their rear ends all along.

Tonight, he intended to find out everything he could about the man.

So, Kevin Harmes began by researching all homes and other properties owned by the filmmaker. There were so many cars and houses that Kevin felt sick as he did his work, but he tried not to let it get to him. What it must be like to have so much money at one's disposal!

The man owned, according to the Department of Motor Vehicles, seventeen cars and three motorcycles. Among the vehicles there were two Porsches, a limousine, and several other foreign jobs, a couple of Harley-Davidsons, and a yacht. Miles March had a pretty impressive collection of rides.

As for homes, the list was astounding. He could see properties owned in the state, and he found six: two in Los Angeles, one in Bakersfield, another in Sacramento, one in Napa Valley, and another in San Diego. Of course, none of this proved anything, but it did spark confirmation in Kevin's mind that he was on the right track. He made a note to find out about other properties that March owned out of state the following morning. For now, all he wanted to do was learn a bit more personal information about the famous director.

Kevin bookmarked the property page he was studying and began to check into the man's background. It seemed, from what he could tell, that the man 'Miles March' had technically come into existence thirty years prior or so. The man himself was around fifty years of age, so the discrepancy grabbed hard onto Kevin's attention. Who was Miles March before he was Miles March?

The internet and Wikipedia gave him very little to go on. All of the history recorded that Kevin could find began by telling of the man's film career; there was no childhood history, mention of parents, siblings, or friends, nothing. It was almost as though he had suddenly appeared on the face of the earth in his late twenties or early thirties and begun to prosper immediately.

Smash Hit might have been his biggest hit to date, but it was far from being his only hit. A Wiki search of the film revealed the plot spelled out: a serial killer stalks victims in accordance with a film in order to exact revenge on a person from the past. Was *Smash Hit* more true to life than anyone understood? Had Miles March actually put together a movie that told of some personal and private aspects of his life?

Kevin sat back and turned these questions over in his mind. Regardless of the answers, none of them pointed to the director as the perp. The fact that he owned planes and homes was circumstantial; even the fact that he flew one of his planes to each of the cities which murders took place in was circumstantial as well.

Kevin clicked the mouse and brought up the bookmarked property page. He sat back once again and looked it over, scanning the information with his eyes.

He reached up and scrolled down the page, reviewing the information on the screen once more. The last property was the one in Bakersfield; nothing new caught his eye until he reached the bottom of the long page.

To the right at the very bottom of the Bakersfield property was a small orange box with the letters REF in it. Kevin's brow creased, and he scrolled rapidly back up to see if the same orange box could be found beneath all the other California properties, but there was nothing. He scrolled down one more time, and without missing a beat, clicked on the small orange box.

This time a single property page came on the screen. The first thing Kevin took note of was the address. According to the information the property consisted of a home in the old West Adams historic district. It had four bedrooms and two bathrooms, and was currently owned but uninhabited, as it had been for some time. There had been several attempts to buy the property, but the owner refused.

There were two owners listed: Ruth Cannon and Donovan Cannon.

Kevin squinted his eyes and stared at the first name. Ruth Cannon? Why did that name sound so familiar? He clicked to make a new tab and brought up a search page, where he entered 'Ruth Cannon Los Angeles'. If the computer didn't know who she was, no one would.

But the computer did know.

Ruth Cannon was a young actress from 1961 to 1967, and she had been famous for her ear-piercing 'screams of terror', which contributed to the popularity of horror films in those days. A few images of Cannon showed a pretty girl in her late teens or early twenties, and she always had a wonderful smile. Kevin scanned down the page to find there was also information on Wikipedia about the actress; he lost no time in clicking that next.

A brief background was given in regard to the woman, including a life history and short list of films she had been in. It seemed that she dropped out of show business unexpectedly sometime in the late sixties, and never returned. She turned into a hermit, from the looks of things: she denied interviews and parts, and even shut herself away in her 'beautiful, luxurious' Los Angeles home at West Adams. She died in the eighties, leaving behind one son, Donovan, who had been a film student at UCLA before disappearing altogether after her death. The home at West Adams was still in his name, but Donovan Cannon had never made a name for himself in movies.

Once again Kevin sat back to think, his fingertips steepled beneath his chin. Donovan Cannon? Had Ruth left the movies to raise her son in peace, perhaps? That would be his guess, but there was nothing specific on Wiki.

Once more he entered her name into the search, this time adding Donovan's with it. Only one thing came up for Donovan: a short article written in the Times for a couple who wanted to purchase the West Adams home.

The writer of the article discussed Donovan Cannon and asked that he or anyone who knew him please contact the interested couple. Other than that, it was as if the man had fallen off the face of the earth.

Back.on Ruth's Wiki page, Kevin took note of the director who had made her films: Webster Morton. He ran an internet check on the man and discovered that he was still alive and well and living in Los Angeles. Kevin glanced at his watch: eleven thirty. He made a note to call the old man as soon as the sun came up.

For now, he would work on finding out why the Cannon property was referenced on Miles March's property list.

CHAPTER 21

Miles March was enduring the feeling that everything was slowly, but surely, unraveling.

It was late Sunday night, and he was standing, motionless, in the shower in his favorite Los Angeles home. It was his favorite because it had a high cast-iron gate and Rottweilers for security. He could hole up there and sort things out in his mind without interruption, at least for now. He was sure the cops were not completely onto him yet, but they would be, and really soon thanks to Travis Cole, the little jerk down at the airport.

In twenty or so short minutes the little punk had given away one of his favorite secrets: his planes. It was the secret that had kept him safe and free to carry on with his art without interruption. Now they were no longer a secret, and while he knew the planes themselves wouldn't get him caught, he was also aware that their existence would spark questions about his dishonesty. Now the cops knew that he lied about being in LA; he was surprised that they weren't there to arrest him when he stepped off the plane.

But they hadn't been. Only Travis Cole and the news of the police visit and the questions they had asked. Miles had handled himself well; he remained calm and kind the entire time the kid talked. He then excused himself to go to the men's room, where he called his limo driver's cell and told him to take the limo back to the garage; he would be catching a ride with a colleague, he said.

He hung around the airport, nervous on the inside, smooth as silk on the outside. He made small talk with Travis Cole for a half-hour before the kid told him he was off and heading for home. Conveniently, Miles had walked him to the parking lot, where he proceeded to make a big deal of his limo not being there yet, and faking a call to his driver, who he swore he was going to fire when he got home.

During the car ride that Travis Cole gave him, Miles March made a very bad decision— a decision that had him shaking in the shower he was now taking.

They had been driving in the direction of March's 'home'. At least, the direction March had told the young airport employee to go, but neither of his LA homes were anywhere near them. March had been intentionally laid back, making small talk, and even cracking a couple of uncharacteristic jokes. Travis Cole had been completely at ease.

They had turned down a dead-end road, prompting March to apologize for giving the wrong directions. When the young Cole went to turn around he suddenly stopped and apologized to Miles March one more time for speaking to the detectives so freely. March had simply smiled, nodded, and waved it off, right before grabbing the big-mouthed little so-and-so by the throat and squeezing the life out of him right where they sat.

He had loved the panicked look in the kid's eyes while the life was draining out of him, but more than that he loved the fact that he could literally feel the life leaving, and that had been enough to give the psychotic movie maker enjoyment. Even after Travis Cole was dead, March had kept his grip on the boy's neck, not letting go. He had then proceeded to put Travis' body in the small back seat and drive the car to an abandoned lot on the other side of town, and from a nearby café had called a taxi to take him home.

But now he knew there would be serious trouble. Morning was very close, and someone would certainly report the kid missing, and March knew without a doubt that it would light a fire under the rears of those two nosy detectives he had underestimated so drastically.

Miles shut off the shower and donned a spotless white terrycloth robe. He sat on the edge of his bed with his head in his hands, thinking about his next move. He had just begun his true work, after all. The next phase, *Smash Hit 2* and all that was to go with it, was just around the corner. He would not, could not, allow himself to fall victim to the law or the police. His work was far too important for all of that. Besides, he loved what he was doing.

So, what was he going to do? Should he go ahead and attend the studio meeting? He thought so. He looked at the clock: five fifteen in the morning. As soon as his secretary got in he would call her and get his messages; he would decide his next move after that. He was pretty sure that, if the cops had gotten to the little nobody Travis Cole, they had certainly gotten to her.

Miles March lay back on his bed, closed his eyes, and waited.

∞

The telephone began to ring.

Kevin Harmes was still in his office, and the sun was just coming up; it was not quite six thirty in the morning. He had been cooped up in his office sucking on tar-black coffee all night; his joints hurt and his stomach was sour, but he was more than ready to get the day started.

He had researched Miles March, as well as Ruth and Donovan Cannon, most of the night as he waited for the morning so he could call the retired director, Webster Morton. He could find no history on March before the guy's late twenties, and that was a fact that both confused and concerned him. Not only that, he could find nothing to explain why the Cannon property was flagged on March's property lists, but he thought he had a glimmer of a reason: somehow the two were related. Perhaps half-brothers with the same father, or something like that.

Kevin learned quite a bit about the March the world knew and seemingly loved.

He had more than twenty horror films credited to him, and almost all of them were hits at some level. He was loved by fans for his uncanny ability to put the viewer in the shoes of the victim through cinematics and exquisite use of realism and emotion. *Smash Hit* had been one of the most awaited March films of all time due to the fact that he had been on hiatus for two years prior to the making of the film. According to March that time had been spent 'resting and being refreshed'.

He was not married, nor did he have children. He had no criminal history, and seemed to have no relatives to speak of. Harmes knew from the looks of things that the man, at some point in time, had intentionally distanced himself from any relatives, and he had probably done so on purpose.

Suddenly the telephone was answered, interrupting Kevin's thoughts.

"Hello?"

The voice was weak and old, and Kevin thought it might be Webster Morton himself answering the call.

"Mr. Morton?"

There was a pause. "Yes. This is Webster Morton. If this is the press I would ask you to leave a tired old man alone, please."

"Mr. Morton, I'm not press," Kevin replied. "I'm Detective Kevin Harmes with the LAPD, and I am currently investigating the Box Office Butcher murders."

Without hesitation the old man began laughing loudly. Kevin let the laughter run its course, smiling slightly with amusement as he listened. Finally, the old man stopped, coughed for several seconds, and spoke.

"If you think I have been out gallivanting and killing, well, you couldn't be more wrong. I am a sick old man, Detective."

Kevin's smile grew. "No, sir. Not at all. I'm calling because I was hoping you could answer a few questions about one of your actresses in the sixties. Ruth Cannon?"

The phone went silent. Kevin could hear the old man's labored breathing, so he waited. His heart was pounding, but he didn't know why.

"What do you want to know about Ruth?" Morton asked.

Kevin cleared his throat. "Sir, I was investigating a suspect lead and came across her name on some property. I was wondering if you could tell me about her."

"So, you suspect Donovan, do you?"

Kevin was stunned. "You know Donovan? Where can I find him, sir? I have some questions about his connection to Miles March."

The man began to laugh hard once again, followed by another bout of coughing. Kevin was becoming confused; he found nothing funny about what he had just said. Was he dealing with a dementia patient?

"You really don't know what you are doing, do you?"

Kevin cocked his head, as if trying to hear the man more clearly. "Sir?"

"I think you had better come see me," Morton said. "Do you have a pen? I'll give you my address. The sooner we talk, the sooner you are going to be on the right track."

Kevin snatched up a pen and wrote as quickly as the man spoke. In minutes he was grabbing his coat and heading out to the lot to get a car. Something inside of him said he was onto the best lead so far.

He couldn't drive across town fast enough.

R.W.K. Clark

CHAPTER 22

Miles March got off the elevator and stepped into the lobby area. He half-expected to see the police waiting for him, but the only people there were his secretary and the cleaning girl, who was busying herself making a large pot of coffee for the morning visitors. Miles made his way to the reception desk; he decided not to call in first. The best thing he could do at that point was carry on with business as usual.

"Good morning, Melody."

The secretary looked up at him as if she were surprised to see him. "Mr. March! Good morning! I didn't expect you in quite so early."

He offered her a weak smile. "Any messages that I haven't already gotten?"

"Just confirmations on this morning's meeting," she said as she began to shuffle through a small stack of pink slips of paper. "Oh, and the police were here again. For some reason they were under the impression that you were in town, but I let them know you weren't here yet."

"Hmm. Well, I'm sure they will be in touch if they need to speak to me," he said lightly. Inside he wanted to reach across the dumb girl's desk and choke her the way he had Travis Cole. He glanced over his shoulder at the cleaning lady, then pushed the thought from his mind. "I have another meeting clear on the other side of town, and I won't make it back here in time for this one. Let's set up a conference call for this one; just dial me up once all of the others have convened, okay? I'll be waiting."

"Sure thing, Mr. March." She began jotting notes down. "Oh, and the police wanted to know if you had heard from Cory Caine. I told them I hadn't, so I think that's all they wanted anyway."

March nodded as he began to walk back toward the elevator. "Yes, if you hear from them today let them know that I have heard from him. He called me and told me that he decided to stay in San Diego for another week. They should be able to track him down there somewhere, although he didn't tell me where it was he was staying." He pushed the button to go down. "I'll talk to you when the others have convened. Have a good morning."

Once March was safely inside the elevator he let out a long sigh, but immediately began to feel the old, familiar rage building up inside of him. Was he dealing with a bunch of idiots, or what? For a bunch of people who were supposed to be on his 'team' they were certainly all as stupid as they came. No wonder

Detective Harmes had made his way to Travis Cole at the airport; Melody had told him that March wasn't in LA at all.

Miles March opened his mouth wide and began to scream long and hard. He didn't care who heard him; he needed to let the fury out somehow, before it destroyed him. Right before the elevator stopped to let him out he composed himself, straightened his suit jacket, and smiled. He was just in time, too. The elevator opened to a group of employees and actors, all of whom March knew all too well.

"Good morning, Mr. March," they all seemed to say in unison.

He nodded curtly, maintaining his smile. "Have a wonderful day, troops."

Soon he was in his car, driving himself to a hotel across town. They knew him there, and they were the most discreet place he knew. They would rent him a room under an alias, and he would be able to take care of his meeting, and sort out his next course of action, without the threat of questioning, or even arrest, by the police.

As he drove he had one sure thought in his mind: he was going to have to get rid of Detective Kevin Harmes one way or another.

∞

"Ruth Cannon was the catalyst that drove me to horror film fame."

Kevin Harmes sat on a comfortable floral loveseat, a steaming cup of coffee on the small table in front of him. Retired film director Webster Morton was seated about five feet from him in a power wheelchair, an afghan covering his lap. He was frail, white-haired, old, and very, very rich.

"I met Ruthie when she was just sixteen," the old man said. "She had come to chase her star, and I was just getting ready to cast my very first 'screamer'. I was pretty young myself."

Kevin remained quiet. He wanted to hear all the man had to say about the actress and her son, Donovan. But he also had a feeling that Morton would be able to open a door in the investigation that Kevin might otherwise have not seen.

The old man paused and coughed into a handkerchief, his body shaking with each and every cough. After a moment, he then cleared his throat and continued.

"I had put an ad in the Times looking for young talent. My first movie was called *Bloody Good Time*, and I had just received all the funding; I had to cast it, and I had to do it quick." The man paused and a smile came to his face as he recalled the memories. After a moment he jerked himself back to reality. "Ruthie came, tried out, and knocked my socks off. She was attractive, articulate, and had a bizarre ear-piercing scream. Not the greatest actress, but oh, that scream.

"I gave her the female lead and, needless to say, it led to me giving her other future parts," he said. "Yes, she was typecast due to the film genre she was in, but that was no problem for her. She was happy to be working. Then, in late 1967, she suddenly 'ducked out'."

Kevin leaned forward. "What do you mean, 'ducked out'?"

Morton shrugged and frowned a bit. "I had a new film we were going to start working on, and I had planned for her to be in it, as usual. We were almost as famous for working together as we were for the work itself. I called her, left messages, even tried to stop by the West Adams house, but to no avail. Finally, afraid for her life after a full month, I hired a private detective to track her down. She was home the entire time, in hiding. I wrote her a letter, and she wrote back, agreeing to see me, but only me, and me alone."

The man stopped. His eyes seemed to be misting up, and he began to stare out the large window next to him, which overlooked a very well-kept garden. Kevin waited for him to continue, but after a long moment it seemed the old man would not.

"What happened, Mr. Morton?" Kevin finally asked.

Morton took a long, ragged breath, dabbed at his eyes with his hanky, and continued. "When I arrived at her home I soon discovered there would be no talking. At least, not on her part. She had to write to communicate with me because her tongue had been cut from her head."

Kevin could do nothing but stare. The revelation the old man had just given him was the last thing he expected, but his heart had begun fluttering again because the last victim, the old man and former convicted rapist Myron Dennis, had had his tongue cut out as well. There had to be a connection.

"Go on, sir."

Morton took another breath. "Not only that, she was pregnant. Ruthie had been raped while strolling one night; the man had cut her tongue out and told her it was to keep her from talking. I told her we could get her an abortion, which I would pay for it and arrange it, but she was adamant that she would have the child. That child was her son, Donovan."

"Where is Donovan now, Mr. Morton?" Kevin asked.

Morton chuckled. "Before we get to that I should tell you about his life with Ruthie. See, you must understand that I was in love with the girl. She wouldn't abort, so I paid off her house and saw to it that she was financially cared for. I thought she wanted to have the baby so that the rape wouldn't be for nothing, but I couldn't have been more wrong.

"She wanted to have that child to exact revenge on his father, and that was what she did." Morton shook his head and tears began to form once more. "She abused him terribly, from the moment he was born, but just enough to inflict pain; she wanted him to live and suffer more. She burned him, beat him, and who knows what else."

He wiped at his eyes. "I tried to intervene, tried to convince her to let me take the boy, but she refused. Anyway, he lived with her always, enduring the pain she inflicted on him, even through his time in college. Ruthie died during his twenty-fifth birthday weekend. Donovan disappeared after that."

Kevin's heart sank. "Do you have any idea why the West Adams property has a flag on Miles March's property list with the city?"

Morton snapped his head up and quickly smiled at the detective. "Of course. Miles March is Donovan Cannon. I thought surely you had figured that out."

Kevin's head swam, but he tried to ignore it. "How do you know that, sir?"

"When Ruthie died the police first thought it was an accident," he replied. "She had been taking a bath, passed out in the tub, and drowned. She was an excessive drinker, and she liked her pills, so it wasn't a surprise. But then the medical examiner found the bruises around her neck. Before the cops could bring Donny in for questioning he disappeared without a trace.

"At first I thought he might have committed suicide. Understand, I couldn't blame Donny for killing Ruthie; she was a horrid, horrid woman to him. I only wished he had come to me. Years passed, things were forgotten, and then a new director came to me wanting me to invest in his first-ever horror film. I had never seen his face, but I knew his voice: it was Donny."

"Did you confront him?"

Morton began to wheel his chair around, much like a man who could walk would pace. "Of course I did, right away! He admitted it immediately. He told me he used the money from his trust, which he had withdrawn right after her death, to have surgery and change his appearance. He changed his name and went to, and completed, film school in New York City. Now, here he is, and from what I can see Donny has been a very bad young man, Detective Harmes."

Kevin stood and approached the man, who was now stopped and staring up at him. "You have known the killer was March the entire time the Box Office Butcher killings were going on?"

Morton shrugged. "I had my suspicions, but when the last victim, the guy in San Diego, was killed and his tongue cut out? Then I knew it for sure. Donny had found his mother's rapist, the cause of his horrible life. Donny has been planning all of this for a very long time, possibly since childhood. In his mind killing his mother was akin to putting her out of her misery."

Kevin was snowed. He couldn't believe all that he had just learned, and the information overload almost made his head spin. He slowly made his way back to the couch and sat down.

"Are you all right, Detective? Can I get you something?"

Kevin shook his head. In a dazed voice he said, "Did you know March is planning a second *Smash Hit* movie?"

Morton's face went stony, and he shook his head. "No, I didn't. But if that's true and he is, you have a major problem on your hands."

"Yes," Kevin replied with a nod. "It's not about revenge anymore. Now it just tastes good."

R.W.K. Clark

CHAPTER 23

Harmes and Joe Carter sped purposefully along the freeway in silence. Between them sat sheets of paper with a list of all properties owned by Miles March; the two men were going to find him and pay him a visit. So far, Kevin had called every number he had for the man and either reached answering machines or was told he was out, so it was time to talk to the man face to face.

They would visit both Los Angeles homes. Harmes had already contacted the airstrip and was told that, for the first time in recent history, all three of March's three planes were gone: one to Minnesota for a sporting event that evening, and one to Bakersfield for business. As for the third plane's destination, the contact at the airport seemed confused by the log, and Kevin had been unable to get any more information over the phone. The contact did promise to call him back as soon as it was cleared up; all he would tell Kevin for sure was that the plane was gone, but no take off was listed for it.

Beat cops were on the lookout for any of the vehicles registered to him, but Kevin didn't expect much from that. If March was true to form he would have thought ahead enough to have rented a car. Kevin knew that, with the money March had things could be done to elude the law that one couldn't even imagine.

But something inside told Kevin that the man was here. Things felt like they were picking up speed, and the old, excited pitter-pattering of his heart agreed. If things truly were coming to a head, Miles March and his mad ego would certainly not want to miss a thing.

"We'll visit his penthouse first." Kevin's remark broke the silence and pulled Carter out of deep thought.

"What do you suppose makes these crazies think the way they do, Kev?" Carter asked. "And a rich pain in the neck at that."

Harmes thought about it for a fraction of a second. "They have no soul, and a soul is something that all the money in the world can't buy."

The vehicle fell into silence once again until they reached the high-rise that seemed to be March's primary choice of residence. The men lit from the plain, unmarked car and strolled over to a doorman in a burgundy and gold uniform. Kevin made sure to smile at the guy as they approached.

"We're here to see Miles March, please," Carter stated politely.

The doorman smiled back pleasantly. "Mr. March isn't here right now. Even if he were, you would need an appointment."

It was time for the men to flash their badges, and the doorman, whose tag read simply 'Daniel', sobered up immediately.

"Employees of Geneva Residential Developments are bound by contract not to discuss any of the private business or lives of residents, both purchasing or leasing." The man obviously had the statement memorized; it was likely part of some sort of high-end doorman training program, Kevin thought.

He clucked his tongue. "Listen, 'Daniel'. We need to speak to Mr. March regarding those movie murders. You know, the Box Office Butcher case. We just need to know if he's been staying here, because we can't seem to get him by phone. We need to update him on the case."

Carter spoke up. "If he's not residing here currently, we'll just check his Beverly Hills home; no problem."

Daniel's eyes lit up. "Have you arrested a suspect? Mr. March will certainly be pleased about that!"

"We're not really at liberty to discuss it, Daniel." Kevin was watching everything from the building's main entrance to the side guest parking lot as he spoke. "We just need to know if this is where to get a hold of him."

Daniel's eyes shifted from the left to the right, then back to the two men. "He was here, but he went out this morning, and I don't think he'll be back tonight. If you really want to get a hold of him the studio is the place, but I can't be sure."

They glanced at each other, muttered thanks to the doorman, and walked away. "I'll try his cell again. Let's head to the studio; we can hit Beverly Hills after that."

With his free hand Kevin tossed the keys at Carter, and he listened to March's voicemail kick in for the tenth time that day. He left no message; the guy wouldn't call him back anyway, and he knew it.

Miles March was the Box Office Butcher.

∞

Hotel room curtains were always so thick and heavy, and Miles appreciated that greatly whenever a headache came when staying away from home. He had a killer one right then, and the room was in heavy blackness and silence. He had almost vomited trying to get off the phone from the conference call with investors for *Smash Hit 2*, but he managed to say all the right things, and told them he was going for a vacay prior to casting.

He had taken one of his headache pills and pulled the curtains. Now, fifteen minutes later, the sharp stabbing of pain in his skull was beginning to subside, just a little bit. He could see the light at the end of the tunnel.

Miles kept his eyes closed and let his mind wander to the situation at hand. Things were grim, and he wouldn't deny it. But he was safe right where he was. They would be racing all around, trying to find him. The cop had beeped in on the conference call three times, but now Miles had the cell off, and calls from Detective

Harmes were the furthest things from his mind. What he needed now was to rest, to get rid of his headache, and then to wake up refreshed so he could think clearly.

So, Miles March let himself drift off, his mind a blank and his heartbeat normal. He didn't care about his victims, and he didn't care about the future. But he did have confidence in his own ability to continue his work without being impeded by dimwit cops on a mission.

He slept like a baby.

R.W.K. Clark

CHAPTER 24

Halfway between the drive from March's penthouse to Milestone Pictures Studios, Kevin Harmes' cell phone began to chirp loudly. He had just been thinking that maybe March just hadn't gotten to his messages. Maybe he would call back. Maybe his ego had him believing he was above the law, smarter, and would never get caught.

He looked at the screen to his cell to see a number from the precinct: his captain, to be exact.

"Harmes, the body of a young man was discovered on a dead-end street around dawn. Some of the detectives checked his ID, and his family has been notified, but when they went to his job to throw around some questions a couple of his co-workers mentioned that you had paid him a visit. Wondering if this homicide is connected to your case somehow."

"What was the vic's name?" Kevin asked.

The captain cleared his throat. "One Travis Cole, twenty-six. A digital log keeper at the private strips at LAX. Had you interviewed this kid?"

Harmes closed his eyes. He was glad at that moment that he had thrown Carter the keys to the car. "Yeah, yes. We just questioned him regarding March's private plane. He clarified for us that March has three jets, and he gave us items from the log. My gosh. This seals it."

"I take it you're onto March then," the captain assumed. "You're liking him pretty good for the Butcher killings then?"

"He's our guy." Kevin's stomach felt sick over the death of the kid, but he also knew that this sealed it for March. "How was the kid killed?"

"Manual strangulation. Where are you heading now?" The captain was all business. He wanted the sicko off the street as much as Kevin and Joe did.

Kevin dragged the back of his hand across his eyes and inhaled deeply. "Well, we can't get March by phone on any number we have for the man. Carter and I have paid his condo a visit and the doorman said he left first thing this morning. He directed us to the studio, which is where we are headed to now. Oh, by the way: thanks for getting that all-points bulletin out. I'm sick over this guy. We've gotta find him."

"Find him and bring him in."

The phone went dead in Kevin's hand. He turned to look at Carter, disbelief filling his mind. This March guy had totally gone off the deep end.

"They found Travis Cole in his car, strangled," he blurted out.

Carter glanced at him and then put his eyes back on the road and punched the accelerator. "We gotta put a stop to this guy. It sounds like he's lost all control; it seems that he has panicked."

"I'd have to agree."

Kevin put a flashing light on the dash and they sped up even more; they would arrive at the studio in just under ten minutes.

∞

"I'm sorry, Detectives, but as I told you on the telephone, Mr. March left this morning, and he won't be back for two weeks."

Little Miss Melody the secretary had an attitude, and neither Kevin nor Joe had any time for it.

"I thought you said he had a meeting this morning for the *Smash Hit* sequel," Carter pressed.

Melody took her eyes from her computer screen long enough to put her nose in the air at the men. "He came in as soon as I got here this morning and let me know that he would be having his meeting via conference call on his cell. When the meeting had convened I simply dialed him in and left the room."

"Where was he, do you know?" Kevin asked.

The young woman snickered and turned her attention back to her computer. "I do not; he doesn't tell me every move he makes. And besides, even if he had I would not relay the information to you; he signs my paychecks, and I think we have talked enough."

Kevin's arm darted out to the left and he tried the knob on Miles March's office door, but it was locked tight. Melody jumped up, flustered and angry. She ran around the desk and stood between the detectives and the door.

"I think you should leave now," the girl demanded. "This is private property, and I will call security."

Kevin held up one disgusted hand. "Don't bother."

As they waited for the elevator Carter said, "What if he's hiding in the office, Harmes? We going to get a warrant?"

"He's not here. He knows we're on to him," Kevin replied thoughtfully. "Right now we are going to go check out his house in Beverly Hills."

CHAPTER 25

Miles March's eyes snapped open suddenly, but the only thing they could see was the blackness.

The room was dead silent, and the first thing that entered his still-waking mind was 'Where the heck am I?" He had just dreamed that he was in a cell, and he was going to prison, where he would be executed. The feelings he felt in the dream were still real to him, and they were miserably strong.

"Wha —"

He sat upright, his back straight and rigid. He tried to listen for any sounds, and as he peeled his ears he remembered. He was in the Duchess Arms Hotel on the top floor. He was safe.

He flung his legs over the side of the bed, flipped the lamp on, and then staggered to the bathroom. As he used the toilet he yawned and remembered his headache; it was nothing but a memory now. He smiled with relief.

Time to turn the cell on. While he waited for it to boot he also flipped on the television, right to a news channel featuring a helicopter view of Travis Cole's car and the surrounding police squad cars and crime scene tape. It was real, and it was happening now. But he didn't feel an ounce of fear anymore, just determination.

He watched the news, entranced and exhilarated. How could he have ever thought that offing the Cole kid was a bad choice? This was like a trailer for a new movie, a teaser for the audiences, a taste for the masses.

He would be sure to add it into the script for *Smash Hit 2*. Maybe the first murder, the film's prologue, would have the killer hitchhiking, and…

His phone chimed. He looked down to see he had a few voicemails and a couple of texts, one being from Melody, his secretary. Time to start playing.

Police here again. Said they are looking for you. Asked questions, but I said nothing. Call ASAP.

The other text was from Kevin Harmes.

Left voicemails. Need to ask you some questions regarding your last flight in. Please call.

Next, he looked at his missed call log. One from Melody at Milestone and nine from the cop's number. He recognized it now; he had spoken to the guy enough.

Miles dialed in the direct number to Melody's desk.

"Thank you for calling Milestone Pictures, Mr. March's office. How can I help you?"

She sounded smooth as silk. Obviously the girl had smartened up. "Melody, this is Mr. March. Now, what's all the drama about?"

"Oh, Mr. March!" She sounded relieved. "The detectives were here to ask if either you or I had heard from Cory at all, and they wanted to know if you were still in Los Angeles, but I told them I couldn't divulge office information. That one policeman tried to open your office, but it was locked, thank goodness."

Yes, they were onto him now. This could be a lot of fun. This could be the biggest afterparty of all time.

"Yes. I've spoken to Cory. We are going to have a meeting regarding the sequel." The lie rolled easily off his tongue. "The authorities still want me to pull the movie, and they want me to halt production of number two until the killer is caught."

She seemed very appeased. "Now, Melody, I am leaving. As of this second, consider me gone. I'm going for my little pre-production tryst, and I expect not to hear a word from you or anyone else, capiche?"

Soon he had her agreeing and hanging up so she could go on with business as usual. He disconnected the call and sat in silence for a bit. It was important that he take things a single step at a time, and that he take each step carefully.

Next, he dialed the number for the doorman's station at his high-rise.

"Corporate Palms by Geneva Residential, how may I help you today?"

The voice on the other line was that of a young man, and the younger, newer doormen acted more like bellboys to the residents. He knew the kid on the phone wouldn't know if the cops had paid his penthouse a visit. He would need to speak to one of the old-timers.

"To whom am I speaking, please?" March asked.

"This is Dustin Wyeth."

March smiled at the kid's innocent-sounding voice. "Thanks, Dustin. This is Miles March, and I own the penthouse."

"Yes, Mr. March!"

"Tell me, Dustin," March continued. "Did you happen to be the man on the main entrance at any time today?"

"One moment." The young man paused for a moment, but quickly returned. "That would be Daniel; he's on until six this evening."

Perfect! Daniel and March had formed something of a loose friendship since he had purchased the penthouse. He would let Miles know if absolutely anything, no matter how minor, was amiss.

"Could you put Daniel on the phone for me?" He asked. "I'm expecting a delivery, and I need him to deal with it hands-on for me."

"No problem, sir," Dustin replied eagerly. "Please hold."

March began to whistle along with the music playing through the phone as soon as it came on. It seemed all concern had left him, and it well should have. He had a plan, and it was unconquerable. As long as he took things slowly and with great timing and caution, he would be able to create his second masterpiece: Part 2.

He was both happy and excited, if not a bit manic.

"This is Daniel, Mr. March. How can I help you today?"

March immediately turned on the charm. "Hello, Daniel. I hope all is well. Listen, I should have told you when I left, but I am expecting a couple of visitors; they are supposed to be bringing me a package that is very important. Has anyone been by for me?"

"Why, yes, sir! Two detectives came by with news about the suspect in those murder killings, but neither of them said anything about a package. No one else has been here." The doorman went silent to give March a chance to respond.

"Well, then, they haven't received it yet," March bluffed. "Quite upsetting. I needed that by tomorrow. Oh, well! And as far as the police go, did you happen to get their names? I'll call them right away."

Daniel put him on hold and returned shortly with the information, which March didn't really need. Important to play off even the smallest, most seemingly insignificant things. He made sounds into the phone as if he were writing down the number, but he already had the number. He wasn't lying; he would be calling Detective Harmes very soon.

When the call was over Miles stared at his phone for some time, playing and replaying the next steps of his plan over and over in his mind. It was important to get it right. It was important that all players get their cues and their parts down to a tee.

He waited another half-hour before calling Kevin Harmes, who picked up right after the first ring.

"Miles, this is Detective Harmes. Thank you for returning my call."

March smiled; this guy was full of it. "What can I do for you? I would have called sooner, but I'm a very busy man, you know."

"Where are you?" Kevin asked.

Miles chuckled heartily. "Where are you, Detective?"

"We had just pulled up to your Beverly Hills property when you called."

More chuckling. "So, you have basically made the rounds, then?"

"Except for your other homes," Kevin said. "Police at those cities are checking as we speak."

Miles thought for a brief second about how smart he had been to have one of his private pilots take off in his third jet. It had cost him an atrocious amount of shush money, but it was done. The plane was sitting at his own private airstrip, hidden from view and waiting patiently for him to arrive.

"I'm not worried about my other homes," Miles said sarcastically. "I'm on vacation, you see."

Kevin's mind was spinning. "Turn yourself in, March. It's over. I know it, and you know it. Don't you think you have done enough to make up for the pain you suffered in your life? Don't you think you have gotten every last ounce of revenge you could possibly get?"

March's eyes narrowed, and his voice took on an air of suspicion. "What are you talking about?"

"Come on, man," Kevin shot out. "The movie, the identical murders. This was all about your mother and her rapist, and the abuse you suffered at her hand, isn't it, Donny?"

March disconnected the call. His heart was pounding, and now he had begun to sweat. How had this lousy little gumshoe traced his history? The jerk had been busy all right. Now he was pissed. It looked like he was going to have to slightly alter the ending of this movie.

Miles March dialed Kevin's cell again.

"I knew you'd call back, March," Harmes greeted.

March paused. "So, what do you want from me?"

"I want you to turn yourself in, Mr. March," he replied gently. "I want you to take responsibility for the lives you have taken. And I want you to tell the world why."

Miles rose and began to pace around the dimly lit hotel room. It took him a few minutes to alter and perfect his plan. Once he had it all lined up in his head he spoke.

"Meet me tomorrow night at nine," he said in a low, angry voice. "You alone. If I see anyone else I'll duck out and you'll never find me. I need to get things off my chest before I'm arrested."

"You know I can't..."

"No!" March spat. "No, Detective. You meet me, and do it alone, or I promise you, I'll disappear and you'll never find me. I can also promise you that I will never stop what I have begun until I'm finished."

Kevin thought for a second. "Fine. What's the address?"

Miles March smiled as he rattled off the number and street. He repeated his instructions for the cop twice, reassuring him that he would act if Harmes didn't comply. They would meet the following night at nine at his old house, the house he had shared with his tongue-less, violent excuse for a mother.

Good; that would give him plenty of time to get the plane packed and ready.

∞

Kevin Harmes let his hand, with cell phone in it, drop to his lap. He simply stared down at it for several seconds, thinking and trying to calm his heart. Finally, Joe Carter pulled him back to reality.

"So, what's the plan?" Joe asked.

Kevin turned to him. "I'm meeting him at nine tomorrow night. We need to make plans to apprehend him, but we have to be careful. He wants it his way, and that's how he's gonna get it."

Carter started the car and began to pull away from the iron gate of the Beverly Hills house drive. "Whatever you say, boss. I'm with both you and your plan."

The two detectives headed back to the precinct in silence.

R.W.K. Clark

CHAPTER 26

Nine o'clock was quickly approaching, and Miles March was beside himself with eagerness.

He was upstairs, in the home his mother had reared him in. There was an attic window which faced out to the front yard and long drive. An iron gate blocked the entrance to the drive, but he made sure the gate was open for his little friend, as he had come to refer to Kevin Harmes in his head. When Kevin arrived March would be able to see, literally for blocks, whether or not he had brought other cops. If he had, March would be long gone before Harmes even crossed the gate's threshold.

He sat back against the wall and glanced at his watch: seven thirty. He would sit exactly where he was until the time came, just in case Harmes decided to come a little early. There was no way they could trap him; he knew more about getting out of this house unseen than most people knew about their own brand of underwear. He was on top of his game.

He glanced around the attic; the space was still full of dusty, moldy items that had been here for as long as he could remember, as well as things he had put here for storage over the years. Most all of it either reminded him of his mother or came directly from her; he hadn't been able to stand the sight of the stuff for years, but he couldn't bear to part with any of it. So, he kept it safely here, in this massive dungeon of a house, which had served as his pseudo-prison for much of his life.

The sun was still shining a bit, and now its evening rays were coming through a circular window across the room. They hit a box tucked in a corner marked with writing: 'Donny', the box said in black marker. The writing was Ruth Cannon's, and just looking at it made him want to vomit.

March crawled across the filthy floor on his hands and knees. When he reached the box he simply stared at it; he had noticed it many times over the years of his life, but he had never opened it, never attempted to see what was inside. Something in his soul always kept him from touching things that were his mother's, or even bore her writing. Even after she was dead the abuse he had suffered at her hands had managed to control him, even to this day in many ways.

But now he felt the old anger boiling up inside of him. He had let that woman control him to this extent? Had he really never opened this box because he was afraid of her still? What was he afraid would happen? Would she come back from the dead and cut him and hurt him? Bull!

March reached out and took a hold of the dust-covered cardboard container. He pulled it until it was right in front of him, and he stared down at his own fingerprints, which had smudged the thick filth which had built up on top. The box was taped shut, and his name, 'Donny', was written across the front, unharmed. Suddenly, he had to know, needed to know, what was inside.

March reached inside of his jacket and pulled out his brand-new filet knife. With the twin prongs on the tip of the blade he began to cut through the tape which secured the box. He worked slowly, reveling in the task as though it were his mother's flesh, and he was getting to be the one to do the slicing after all these years.

The tape across the top flaps gave way, and March began cutting at the corners, breaking the seal that was made by the tape around the edges of the box. When the seal was completely broken the flaps of the box gave, popping up slightly to signify that it was open.

March dropped the filet knife to the floor, where it lay forgotten for the time being. He stared at the box with a weak heart. The abused boy living inside of him was trembling with fear at the thought of opening the box; his mother always let him know that touching her belongings would result in terrible punishment. But she wasn't here; he could do what he pleased if he could just work up the courage.

He clamped his eyes shut like a child and grabbed on to one of the flaps, pulling it open. With that done, it seemed that his courage returned. March opened his eyes and quickly opened the remaining three flaps.

Photo albums filled the box to brimming. They were neatly stacked, one on top of the other, until they were flush with the top of the box. The first album he laid his eyes on was emblazoned with the year his mother died; the one next to it, the year before. He slowly began to remove the albums one at a time; each one had a year written on it, and they were stacked in order. He continued to fish them out, and the last one he pulled from the box bore the year he was born. Had Ruth Cannon actually been hoarding keepsakes of him? Photos of a boy she never loved?

He decided to start at the beginning, which was the album of the year he was born.

March ran his hand lovingly over its cover. For the first time in his life he felt hope, or at least what he thought was hope. It was a foreign emotion, but he could label it no other way. Maybe all the abuse over the years really did stem from some kind of affection, and he had simply misread her motives. Perhaps she had really been doing the best she could all along…

He flipped open the cover.

The first photo was alone beneath the plastic sheath which held it down. It was a picture of him as an infant; he was in a tiny bed, surrounded by others just like it. It was obvious to March that he was in a hospital nursery unit when the photo was taken. The sight of it made him smile slightly, and it made his heart flutter.

But when Miles March turned the page, the truth hit him like a truck hitting a brick wall at full speed.

The next page showed him around the same age, but this time he was at home. He was in a bassinet, but he recognized a red chair sitting to the right of the baby bed. That chair was still in the bedroom that had been his mother's.

He was lying naked on top of a blue blanket. The photo was old, and the colors were a bit off due to the poor technology of the day, but he could still identify them. His tiny, squirrelly baby body was bare, and he was gazing off at some unseen thing. Two long, red, angry cuts ran down his legs, one on each thigh.

Beneath the photo a date was written in Ruth Cannon's handwriting: he had been two days old.

The page opposite held another single photo. The date beneath this one was three days later. He was on his stomach, and a large 'X' was cut into the soft flesh of his baby back. Tears began to well up in Miles March's eyes, and rage began to fill his soul. That woman had started with him almost the second he was born.

His eyes were wide and his mouth hanging open as he flipped through the pages, slowly at first, then faster and faster. By the time he was finished with the first one he was both dumbfounded and enraged. He flung the book into a dusty corner and grabbed the second one, which he was through with in less than a minute. Soon he was furiously turning pages and throwing the albums almost faster than he could get his hands on the next one.

He was half through when the tears began to fall silently down his angry and confused face. Not only had the woman abused him his entire life, she had documented each and every incident for her own pleasure. As he aged in the photos it became obvious that he was sleeping when they were taken. She had cut him and then taken pictures when he fell asleep, and she had done this up until the abuse stopped and she was dead.

When he was finished with the last album Miles March threw his head back and screamed at the top of his lungs. He stood and kicked the empty box which the albums had been in; it flew across the room and into the far wall, producing a cloud of dust upon impact. He was blind with fury, kicking everything in sight, punching anything and everything that was at fist level.

"You rotten bitch!" he cried. "You never loved me! You hated me!"

He began to rip and tear at other boxes, flinging them to the floor. He punched a dressmaker's dummy and sent it flying. Clothing and wigs were all over the floor by the time he ran out of breath, and he had to stop and bend over to get his wits about him once again.

March began to cry in earnest then. All of the strength left his legs and he sat down hard on the dirty floor, where he sobbed for a full ten minutes. Finally, he dragged the sleeve of his jacket across his face to dry his eyes, then he looked at his watch: fifteen minutes until nine.

Kevin Harmes would be arriving soon.

March used his hands to scoot himself across the dusty floor and back into his original position by the window. He didn't have time to whine about Ruth. He had to pay close attention to what was going on now. It was important to keep himself safe from any additional police that Harmes might try to bring with him, and March was convinced that the cop would, indeed, be in the company of his co-workers. It would be insane for him not to be. Miles March intended to have a bit of fun with the detective.

He was going to show the man exactly what it was like for Donovan Cannon to grow up with Ruth.

∞

After receiving the call from March requesting Harmes to meet him at Ruth Cannon's old abandoned home, Kevin sat with Joe Carter and their captain in the captain's office. Plans had to be made to meet up with the madman, and the captain wanted to keep Harmes safe at all costs. But Kevin Harmes knew that if March was tipped off on the police presence it would compromise the arrest.

"Sir, if he thinks even for a fraction of a second that you guys are anywhere around, he is going to bolt," Kevin was saying. "And he has the means to avoid arrest indefinitely, sir."

Captain Harvey Meyer was pacing behind his desk, his hands clasped behind his back. "Harmes, if you think I'm going to send you into this so he can take you out like a fish in a barrel, you're dead wrong, forgive the pun."

Carter spoke up. "Sir, if I may. We have been working this from the beginning, and the facts we have uncovered point to this sicko. I think, while dangerous, Harmes going alone, at least initially, is the only way."

Captain Meyer stopped and looked at Carter, his head shaking 'no' adamantly.

Harmes took a deep breath. "Listen, Captain. I'll go at nine; I'll be wired up so you can monitor all interactions. Keep backup out of the perimeter, at least out of sight, until I give the word. Then you can send them in running. But if he sees you, he's going to run before I even get to the front door. I need a half-hour to get a full confession; just give me thirty minutes, please."

Captain Meyer sat at his desk and gazed out the window as he considered Harmes' suggestion. After a moment he looked at the detective with stony eyes. "Okay. I'll go for it. But if it even sounds like there is a problem before he confesses, we're coming in, even if you don't give the word. So, what's the word going to be?"

"Simple," Harmes said with a grin. "Action!"

Meyer smiled back. "Okay. So, let's go over the plan and make it solid. At eight thirty you head over there.

We will be four blocks away in plain cars; we hear you, we come. If all sounds kosher, we won't come until you give the word. Agreed?"

Both Carter and Harmes nodded and said in unison, "Agreed."

The rest of the time that day, up until it was time for Harmes to leave, was spent prepping the officers who would be on the arrest team and getting Kevin ready for his wire. He had to shower and shave his chest, and then he had to be rigged up. By eight o'clock that evening, Harmes' heart began to pitter-patter; it was getting close, and his body knew it better than he did.

He was nervous. He didn't want to let on, though, and give Captain Meyer any reason to want to change the tactics they had agreed on, so he maintained a calm quiet exterior, even cracking a few jokes and talking sports with the rest of the guys. But the fact was, all Kevin Harmes could think about was the level of sickness Miles March had demonstrated to the world. What would keep him from simply slitting Harmes' throat? Maybe that was his plan anyway.

But something inside the veteran detective said otherwise. Harmes thought he knew exactly why March wanted to spend time with him, and it had nothing to do with killing him outright. If he stayed true to psycho form he would want someone to brag to about what he had done, and there was no better person to hear the boasting than the cop who had been trying to bring him down.

So, with all those thoughts in mind, Kevin Harmes and his brand-new wire were ready to get the show on the road. At twenty minutes past eight he was armed, had his jacket on, and had his car keys in hand. He was sitting at his desk calming himself with deep-breathing exercises and listening to Captain Meyer go over the plan again and again, with Joe Carter's help. Harmes found that he wanted to strangle both of them just to make them shut up. He put up with it for five more minutes before standing and holding his hands up to them palms out.

"Enough," he said calmly. "I've got this; I'm going to be fine." He turned to Meyer. "You just have the men in place, and all of this is going to turn out just the way it should."

Both Meyer and Carter studied him for a moment before offering up silent nods. Then Harmes turned his back to them both and left the squad room. It was time to get a move on. As he let the glass door swing shut behind him, he could hear the captain getting everyone ready to leave. Things would be fine.

The drive to West Adams would take just under thirty minutes. Harmes was sure March wouldn't mind if he was a few minutes early. The thought made Kevin smile; here he was, getting ready to meet with a serial killer and his thoughts were about punctuality. He even gave a nervous chuckle before shaking off as much of his stress as he could.

"Okay," Kevin said as he took a GPS-prompted left. "I'm getting ready to turn down the street to the house. I hope you guys are in place."

He drove for about ten seconds, and then he arrived. It was dark, but he could see that the heavy iron gate was open invitingly. He stopped the car and looked at the property; there were no lights on in the massive home whatsoever, and there were no cars or any other sign that Miles March might be inside. For a fraction of a second Harmes felt something like relief; maybe the sicko had changed his mind.

But Harmes didn't think so. No, this sicko would want to make sure to confront his pursuer. The ego of criminals like this one didn't allow them to scrimp when it came to attention and recognition, and Harmes was pretty sure that March led the pack when it came to ego. Who makes a movie and then commits murders according to what they have created? A major egoist, that's who.

Kevin pulled the plain squad through the gate slowly. He had no sooner crossed the threshold completely than the gate began to close behind him, confirming his suspicions: Miles March, aka Donovan Cannon, was waiting inside, and he had made sure he was in control of everything.

"I just pulled in, and the gate is closing behind me, even though the house is dark." Harmes was trying to keep his guys posted as much as he could. They needed to know about a closed wrought-iron gate, which was for sure. "I'm going to park and get out; after that you won't be hearing anything intentional from me."

Harmes pulled to the right and put the car in park, keeping his eyes glued to the house and peeled for any movement whatsoever. Everything seemed perfectly still. He shut off the ignition and put his hand on his service revolver. March never said anything about him coming unarmed.

Kevin got out of the car and closed the door with his hip. It was right at that moment that he noticed the front door; it was open wide, and there was nothing but darkness within. His heart began to pound; he felt like he was in a horror movie himself. He wasn't sure his heart could take it.

With his gun out and up, Kevin began to slowly approach the mansion. He was taking slow steps, moving his gun from the left to the right and back again as he neared the building. "Hello?" he hollered. "March? I'm here! It's Harmes, and I'm alone!"

Kevin went silent as he listened for some type of response, but his words were met with silence. He began to step forward again when he noticed that his gun hand was trembling. It wouldn't do at all to let March see his nerves or any kind of fear, so he began to breathe in and out deeply to get the tremors under control.

When he reached the giant wrap-around porch he took the first step then stopped and listened. Nothing but rustling foliage found his ears. Squinting in the darkness he looked from the left to the right, then back at the front door. Harmes began to climb the steps again, so slowly you would think he was a crippled old man trying to gain his footing.

Now he was on the porch, and he was satisfied that no one was outside with him. The streetlights were illuminating a large staircase inside the house, which became clear after he was right in front of the door. Kevin took a deep breath and entered the house.

"March!" he yelled once again. "I'm here, just like you wanted! Do you want to talk? Here I am!"

Once again, his words were met with silence. Harmes continued to look around, doing the best he could to see in the darkness, and aiming his gun wherever his eyes went. He could hear the old place creaking around him, and the sound sent chills up and down his spine.

Suddenly, Harmes heard a loud bang! It seemed to come from upstairs somewhere, and he jerked both his eyes and his gun in the direction from which it came. Right at that moment came the sound of a metal object bouncing off the floor. Harmes automatically turned in the direction of the noise, both hands on his gun now. His hands were shaking as though they were leaves in the wind.

Something came down on his head with great force. His gun flew from his hands, and he dropped to his knees. After a split-second he crumpled to the floor face down, completely unconscious.

"Welcome, Detective Harmes," Miles March said in the darkness as he closed and locked the front door. "Thanks for coming alone."

CHAPTER 27

Kevin Harmes had a headache.

He was in a dark cloud, or so it seemed to his mind, and he was trying to snap out of it. His eyes fluttered open, and all he could see was a dim light off to his left, which managed to illuminate the surrounding objects, but all he could make out were dark, blob-shaped forms. He shook his head a bit, trying to clear it, but the shaking made his head throb worse.

"Anyway, as I was saying, I appreciate you listening so patiently."

It was Miles March's voice. Kevin closed his eyes, then opened them again, blinking rapidly. The details of his surroundings were clearing up now. He was in a room filled with boxes and chests, and a dressmaker's dummy was lying on the floor, its missing arm a few feet from it. There were windows in the room, but they were covered. As his vision cleared Kevin could tell by the looks of things that he was in what appeared to be an attic or other storage area. Both his hands and feet were bound to the arms and legs of an old chair.

Standing before him, a sick smile on his face, was Miles March. Dangling from one hand, which he held out before him, was Kevin's wire. With his other hand he held his forefinger over his grinning lips, signifying that Kevin needed to be quiet.

"You've been so generous in listening to my story," March continued. "I appreciate it; really, I do."

Kevin glanced down and saw that his shirt was hanging in tatters from his body. It was freezing cold in the room, and goosebumps covered his flesh. He looked back up at March.

"I appreciate you sharing, but I might need you to repeat a few things," Kevin said. "I guess I was spacing out."

He knew right away that March had continued carrying on some kind of one-sided conversation after knocking him out. He had likely done so to stall the troops. Kevin watched the man's face for a change of expression, and it came in the form of his broad smile disappearing all at once.

"So, where are they, Kevin?" he asked.

It was Kevin's turn to smile. "Not here, obviously, but not far. They won't come until I say."

March's smile returned. "Good."

His attention turned to a few large piles of what appeared to be photo albums. They were neatly stacked right next to him, as if they were just waiting. Kevin patiently waited as well.

"My mother was an actress, but I'm sure you know that," he began. "I told you once, but I would never tire of telling it again. It's good to have someone really listen."

He paused and tucked the wire into his jacket, then withdrew a sinister-looking filet knife. He waved it around for Kevin's benefit a couple of times, then bent down and picked up one of the albums.

"Yes, she was an actress," he continued, "but she was also a cruel woman of astronomical proportions. You see, she hated me from the time I was born. She hated me with a violence and a vengeance. See for yourself."

March strode over to Kevin and knelt before him, placing the album down on his lap. He opened the cover for Kevin to see. "That baby? That's me. What a cutie pie!" The man's use of baby talk gave Kevin the creeps. The guy had completely snapped.

Now March sat down cross-legged on the floor, making himself comfortable. "Would you ever hurt such a precious innocent? Would anyone you even know?"

Kevin shook his head, and March flipped the page.

"Well, Ruth Cannon would." March said.

Harmes looked down once again to see the same baby with vicious slashes going down both tiny legs.

"Feel free to browse," March said lightly. With deft movement he used his knife to cut the ropes that bound Kevin's hands as he stood up, and he nodded toward the album to clarify what he wanted Kevin to do before he began pacing. As he spoke he jabbed his knife here and there in the air to enunciate his words. "She was a 'scream queen'. They loved her because she could scream like no other, and it didn't hurt that she was beautiful. But then everything changed for her."

He paused for effect, looking dazedly around the room, then back to Kevin. "She was leaving the studio one night and was raped. But the so-and-so didn't just rape her. He cut her tongue from her body for a souvenir. Left her pregnant with me. Film career ruined. She despised every breath I took."

Immediately, Kevin's thought went to the last victim of the Box Office Butcher killings, Myron Dennis. His tongue had been cut out, too, and he had been a convicted rapist. Kevin knew he had been the rapist who committed the crime against Ruth Cannon.

"She hated me so much that the one thing that made my presence tolerable to her was to make me hurt."

While March spoke Kevin slowly flipped through the album, and when he finished March put another one in front of him. The number 1969 was on its cover, and Kevin assumed it was a year. He opened it and began turning pages.

"So, she would cut me," March continued, "with a knife almost just like this one. If I annoyed her, or talked too much, or spoke at all. Sometimes if my breathing was too loud."

Kevin could hear agitation building in March's voice. "It went on, and on, and on, and on. I thought it would go on my entire life. I tried so hard to make her love me. I sat quietly; I rubbed her stinking feet. All she would ever do was cut, and cut, and cut!"

He grabbed yet another album and threw it in Kevin's direction, making him jump. The album on his lap fell to the floor just as the one March threw struck the wall behind him. Kevin watched as the man began to throw the albums all around the room frantically.

"I even got into movies," he was saying. "I hated movies, but I did it thinking she might love me, finally! But no!"

He ran full force toward Kevin, stopped in front of him with the knife out, then turned around and strolled calmly back to where he had been standing. "I couldn't take it anymore, so I gave the dirty wench a taste of her own medicine and got rid of her. I put her out of her misery once and for all. But then! Then, I got the idea for my masterpiece."

March went quiet. He was staring at the ceiling again, this time his eyes calm and clouded over with what appeared to be contentment. He was smiling, and he even began to hum.

"Mr. March," Kevin began, "I'm sorry—"

March hissed and swung his arm in Kevin's direction, the knife jerking in his hand in a sinister fashion.

"Shut up, piggy," March spat. "You have no idea! You have nothing to be sorry about! I'm a grown man, and what I have done to make things right is something you will never, ever understand! I'm talking right now, not you! Me!"

Kevin clamped his mouth shut and nodded. Miles March watched him, and after a minute it seemed he had calmed himself. He continued with his story.

"So, I killed her. Then, one day, I decided that if she couldn't love me when she was alive, she would love me from Hell." He looked down at the blade of his knife and moved it around randomly, watching as the light coming from the lantern in the far corner bounced off it playfully.

"I would make a movie about all of the cutting, about the things she did to me," he said wistfully. "But in the movie I would be able to have it done to other people, and maybe it would help me to deal with the blackness inside. But all it made me do was want to do the cutting myself, so I did. Then, I found Myron Dennis, and I knew I could make all things right with my mother, so I wrote in the murder of a character just like him. That way, when the movie was done, I could do all the cutting for myself. I could show Ruth that I am a real man."

He looked up at Kevin. "Do you get it yet?"

All Kevin could do was nod, hoping to appease the killer. March watched the gesture and began to laugh, then stepped forward to where Kevin sat. He pulled a rope out of his pocket and began securing the detective's wrists once again.

"I think you get the point of the pictures," he said as he worked. "I don't think you need to see any more."

When he was finished he stepped back as if to admire his own work. When he was three feet away he pulled the wire from his pocket and gently disconnected it from the battery pack and dropped it to the floor. Kevin's heart sank; he knew his men wouldn't be able to tell it had been disconnected right away.

"Now, I want you to know how it felt to be me growing up."

He approached Kevin slowly, kneeling before him once again. March held the knife up in front of the cop's face. "These little prongs on the end? They hurt like you won't believe."

Kevin began to squirm as March put the knife blade closer and closer to his face. The man was getting off on his fear. Suddenly, he jerked his hand and drew one of the prongs down Kevin's left cheek. Immediately he could feel the warm trickle of blood and it oozed from the stinging slit in his skin. He clamped his eyes shut, but he didn't cry out.

"Oh, not enough to get a rise out of you?" March asked. "Let's try this!"

The man plunged the filet knife into Kevin's thigh right near his knee. Now the detective did more than cry out. He screamed in earnest, and March began to laugh as though he were being thoroughly entertained.

"Yes! That's it! You've captured the pain the character is feeling!"

The pain was causing Kevin to see stars, and blood was seeping through his slacks at an alarming rate. Right at that moment he knew with great clarity that the so-and-so was going to kill him. That had been his plan all along. But how did he expect to get away once the job was done? Where the heck was his backup team?

Now March was dancing in circles in front of him, knife securely in hand. He was humming a cheerful tune, and his steps were sure. This guy was as out of his mind as they came. He spun and whirled to whatever song he was trying to make, and all at once he charged forward and buried the knife in Kevin's right shoulder.

It seemed at that very second that Kevin knew he was going to die.

This time, when March pulled the blade out, he didn't back away. He didn't begin to dance or rant or hum. He simply plunged the knife back into Kevin's body again and again. All at once the detective stopped feeling the pain, and the room began to fade around the edges of his vision.

Then the sirens came.

Kevin Harmes seemed to hear them from wherever his mind was going, and for a fraction of a second he thought the beautiful sound was coming from Heaven. Right then he realized, with something still flickering in the back of his mind, that the stabbing had stopped. Maybe he was already dead.

His eyes fluttered open, and he saw Miles March standing in front of him, the knife in his hand dangling at his side. He was looking toward one of the covered windows, and his head was cocked as if he were trying to pick up a sound only he could hear. The sirens were getting louder, and Kevin's fading mind suddenly realized that his team was coming for him. He weakly turned his head toward the same window March had been staring at. When he looked back Miles March was gone.

Kevin exhaled loudly and tears fell down his cheeks, stinging the wound on the left, as he began to cry. He could register the sirens clearly, and just as he heard tires on gravel he realized they were there to save him. He didn't know what to do, so he began to yell for help immediately.

In less than a minute cops began to flood the attic. One was calling for an ambulance while a couple of them focused on untying the ropes which bound him. Flashlights were flooding the room and causing him to squint and jerk from the brightness.

"Where is he, Kev?" Joe Carter was kneeling right in front of him. "Where did March go?"

Kevin stared blankly. Where had March gone? He had been right there a little bit ago.

Joe quickly looked over his shoulder at a uniformed cop. "We've lost the suspect! Spread out and search every room in the house and every inch of the grounds, pronto!"

Harmes closed his eyes and laid his head back. He was so tired. If he could just take a little nap he would be good as new.

"Kevin! Kevin!"

His eyes opened slowly. "Stay with us, bro," Carter was saying. "The bus is on the way. I need you to stay with me now."

But Detective Kevin Harmes just couldn't keep his eyes open.

∞

When Miles March heard the sirens he knew that his little plan could unravel.

At first, the sound had startled him, and he froze where he stood. But it hadn't taken him long to pull himself back to reality, and he made a run for it in a fraction of a second. He had even forgotten the bloody cop he left behind.

He had run out the back of the house. Miles knew this house and the surrounding property better than anyone on the planet. The house was surrounded by a fairly large patch of dense woods. When he was a child there had been a trail leading through them that ended up at a clearing. In that clearing was a small, makeshift runway which his mother's friend Webster Morton had used often when he was young. Now, his own plane, the smallest of his aircrafts, was waiting there for him, packed and ready. It had been part of the plan all along to misdirect the cops with his planes, and then use one to escape their clutches.

When he got to the edge of the woods there was no obvious trail as there had been when he was young. Now it was overgrown with long grass and reeds. But Miles knew exactly where the head of that trail was, and soon he was running at full speed through the dark woods, his footing as sure as if he had been some kind of nocturnal animal.

When he got to the clearing his plane was waiting, ready and running, prepared fully to take him where he needed to be to get safe. He would fly a short distance to where he had a car waiting, and he would set himself completely free from there.

As he began to get into the plane he turned just in time to see the flashlights; they were coming through the woods. He simply stepped all the way in and secured the door. As he buckled in and the plane began to taxi Miles saw the cops break the tree line.

Seconds later he was soaring through the night sky, away from Los Angeles, and away from the house at West Adams.

∞

"Where else could he have gone?"

Captain Meyer was standing with Joe Carter in a private hospital room. Kevin Harmes had just gained consciousness after having had surgery to repair the damage done by the treacherous filet knife. Now, even in his weakened, pain-pill-induced state, Kevin wanted nothing more than to figure out where the Box Office Butcher could have flown off to. He shook his head in response to the captain's question; it seemed all he had the energy to do at that moment.

Carter spoke up. "With all of his money and resources, he could be anywhere by now."

It had been hours since the bloody attack on Harmes at the West Adams home. He had undergone surgery, went through post-op, and was now lying in a hospital bed bandaged and furious. He had never felt so worthless in his life.

The captain's cell began to chirp loudly.

"Meyer," he answered.

The man's face was as unreadable as stone as he listened to whatever was being spoken into his ear. Kevin lay back on the bed, his eyes half-open, watching his superior and waiting, while Joe Carter picked at a hangnail on his left hand. After a brief moment Meyer grunted, gave a half-hearted 'thanks', and disconnected the call.

"That was Sergeant Warren," Meyer said flatly as he continued to stare at the cellular phone in his hand. "A car belonging to Miles March went over a cliff on Pacific Coast Highway a few hours ago. Emergency vehicles are on the scene now, but it appears that March was in the driver's seat. His body is burnt to a crisp."

Joe stared at Meyer with his mouth open. Kevin shook his head and closed his eyes. His laughter was no more than a sarcastic snicker at first, but then it grew into full blown hysterics.

The sicko of a movie maker would never go to trial. In a final act of defiance Miles March had seen fit to take his own life. Kevin Harmes, patched up from the man's attack, wasn't a bit surprised.

"That's a wrap," he said through his laughter and tears.

R.W.K. Clark

EPILOGUE

The sun, in great oranges and purples, was going to bed, tucking itself neatly into the depths of the sea.

The sand threw tiny darts of light which the dwindling sun bounced off it. Just as the dying rays danced on the water, they danced on the shore. It was breathtakingly beautiful, and there was no place like it anywhere on Earth. It was also quiet; just the sound of the ocean kissing the shore could be heard all around.

The island was off Cuba's mainland, and it was nothing more than a spot in the sea in the grand scheme of things. It was so isolated and bred such a sense of loneliness that those on the mainland had named it 'Oculto Isla Diablo', or Hidden Devil Island. To those who had coined the name, it couldn't have been more appropriate.

Back from the shoreline, amongst the trees and shrubs, was a home. Not overly large, but most certainly comfortable. It had been completed almost a year ago. Now it was warmly lit, bearing the telltale signs of the life abiding within. To the right of the home, at the rear, was a large helicopter sitting in the middle of a clearing.

It was the only way off Oculto Isla Diablo, but there was no reason to leave; Hidden Devil Island was literally… Paradise.

A small window was slightly cracked toward the front of the house to allow the air to circulate as best as it could. From just outside the window the sound of a man's voice could be heard. The man spoke Spanish, just as the person listening was able to. It was a reporter on a television news program, and he was delivering the latest news to the public.

His report consisted of a story on a famous American man who began killing. He had murdered more than seven people that authorities were aware of, then tried to kill a Los Angeles police detective during a meeting. According to the news report, the man, a movie producer and director, had escaped police clutches and disappeared, only to be killed in an automobile accident when he drove his vehicle over a cliff on Pacific Coast Highway in the United States. The newsman ended his report with a smile; no worries for Americans now that the killer was dead.

Suddenly, the television went black. The man who had been watching tossed the remote control on the sofa next to him, then stood and stretched slowly. He then cracked his knuckles and went outside. The beach this time of the evening was one of his favorite places to be in the world.

He left the luxurious house barefoot, and walked across the beach until he was about ten feet from the shoreline. He closed his eyes and inhaled the scents which wafted all around him. There were no smells like these anywhere, either.

When he opened his eyes he thought about the newscast, and it brought a smile to his face. Cory Caine's body had certainly served its purpose. They had been the same height and approximate weight; it would take the authorities a long time to discover the truth, if they ever did. His smile broadened, and he began to chuckle.

Soon, the chuckle turned into a full-blown guffaw. He found it hilarious how stupid they all were, how bumbling. Here he was, comfortable and still rich, a brand-new face, and an even newer name. Oh, yes, things were going to work out perfectly.

He was already nearly done with the screenplay for his next film...

R.W.K. Clark

ENTREATY

My creativity is fueled by readers like you. If you enjoyed this novel, I implore you to please write a review, and share your experience on the retailer's website. The livelihood for authors is fully dependent on reviews, and I must say, it is the largest obstacle as a struggling author that I have encountered. Please tell a friend, tell a loved one about this read. With your help, I will be one step closer to overcoming this obstacle. In return, I thank you from the bottom of my heart, and greatly and deeply appreciate your time and effort.

Humbled, with gratitude,
R.W.K. Clark

ADDITIONALLY

Works by R.W.K. Clark

BOX OFFICE BUTCHER

ISBN-13: 978-0997876758 ISBN-10: 0997876751
ISBN-13: 978-1948312165 ISBN-10: 1948312166
ISBN-13: 978-1948312158 ISBN-10: 1948312158

Psychological Thriller

Box Office Butcher is a psychological thriller murder mystery about a killer who is murdering people in an identical manner as that which is done in a new hit slasher flick. While the premise is similar to that of the popular 'Scream' franchise, readers will find that I have written this in a manner that is actually much different, making it unique in almost every aspect. The bottom line, however, is the same: There is a lunatic killing people out there, and he has to be stopped.

Dubbed 'The Box-Office Butcher' by the press, the killer is committing a couple of killings every weekend, and he isn't doing this in a specific area; he's moving around. This results in Detective Kevin Harmes, of the Los Angeles Police Department, scrambling from here to there and back again to try and keep up. Fortunately, this seasoned cop has some pretty spot-on suspicions of his own. Regardless of this fact, 'The Butcher' manages to keep him on his toes, and miserably so, with the sick game he is playing.

It is important to understand that the killer has a vendetta, and it is very necessary to accomplish it. For him, these murders are rooted in a history of abuse and rage, and he feels the compelling need to take care of the issue, which he has carried around with him his entire life. It is more than simply killing because he's a sicko, or because it's fun, though these are true as well. His actions are essentially a way to make right a past that has, unbeknownst to him, destroyed him from the inside out.

Keep in mind that none of the 'copycat' killings are identical to the one from the film which they are meant to emulate. The Butcher doesn't have the kind of power it would take to make his victims cooperate with a scripted film and still enjoy the spontaneity and horror he is set on sparking and enjoying. With this being said, he is a careful planner, spending both time and money to get the real-life murders as close to the ones on film as he possibly can, and he comes terrifyingly close each time.

The Butcher is a man of means, and this becomes obvious by his ability to move so freely from city to city; obviously, he isn't broke or lacking finances of some kind. This is a point which Detective Harmes picks up on and is vital to his investigation. Unfortunately, the suspects that are on his list all fall into this category at one level or another, so he must do the footwork to weed them out.

The Butcher is a very sick man, and it was important to drive this home through a variety of methods. I wrote about him watching the scenes over and over again, which he was preparing to emulate, even though it was obvious he knew them like the back of his hand. I also added an element of sexual stimulation when he watched, as an added bonus pointing to his psychosis.

The hardest part of this work, for me, was keeping the real killer's identity from being given away during the investigation. It was difficult to give some hints here and there while still shining the spotlight on another, as a distraction. There was a fine line here that couldn't be crossed, at least, not immediately, and it was like a balancing act to walk that line. It helped to have The Butcher intentionally raising suspicion on other suspects who could reasonably be the killer that he actually was.

Why is Kevin Harmes so obsessed? Because he believes that every wrong turn he has taken, and each incorrect assumption he has made, is being orchestrated by The Butcher, and this enrages him. As an experienced detective, the fact that a criminal like The Butcher knows that Harmes will buy his bluff and veer off in another direction is bothersome, to say the least. He almost takes this as an assault on his policing ability. Sure, people are dying, but for Harmes, that's just the tip of the iceberg. The Butcher is also basically making fun of the cops, running them around from city to city in confusion, like small children trying to catch a balloon filled with helium, but is always out of reach.

As can be expected, as the story goes on, Harmes finds little tidbits here and there which begin to clear the fog covering The Butcher's identity. Everything begins to make sense, and sure enough, the killer is someone who has been on his suspect list all along. The person has misdirected and lied to the point that it should have been obvious from the beginning. By the time Harmes is ready to nab the guy, he finds that he isn't a step ahead at all; rather, The Butcher already has a plan for this, as well, and it includes Kevin Harmes.

Box Office Butcher, with all difficulties aside, was a fun novel to write. The murder mystery genre label which it falls under afforded me much freedom; I just had to sort my way through what was believable and what would appear to be smoke and mirrors to the reader. I had to reconcile the two to each other without giving away The Butcher's identity too quickly, and hopefully, I accomplished this properly. I also had a lot of fun with The Butcher's past, though it was horrid. The abuse the guy went through at the hands of his own twisted, sick mother are enough to cause anyone to almost understand how someone could go to the kinds of extremes that this killer did.

PASSING THROUGH

ISBN-10: 1948312018 ISBN-13: 978-1948312011
ISBN-10: 1948312093 ISBN-13: 978-1948312097
ISBN-10: 1948312107 ISBN-13: 978-1948312103
ISBN-10: 1948312115 ISBN-13: 978-1948312110

Psychological Thriller

I believe that writers and novelists, as in any profession, change and grow over the timespan that they work and produce. Any of my readers and fans who are familiar with my books and the 'genres' they are 'classified' under are able to recognize the point I am making. Authors' characters get more detailed and personal; descriptions get a bit more intense, as do emotional scenes of any kind. I have also found, for myself, that with each and every book I put out, I seem to get a bit more 'guts' about what I am willing to put down on paper. For instance, I'll admit it, in the beginning, writing a detailed love scene was something I dreaded, but I do much better now, and I'm getting much more comfortable, with experience, in that particular area. This, of course, is just one example.

'Passing Through' is my latest release, and it is the third book I have written that I would call a psychological thriller. The first was 'Brother's Keeper', and when I wrote that I thought it was a bit much. 'Passing Through' is on an entirely different level, however, not just in its depth and explicitness. Now, I realize that there will be fans out there who will love this book; perhaps it will surprise them, and they will find it will be just what they were waiting for from me. Others, though, are going to despise it.

'Passing Through' was very difficult for me to write for a number of reasons, but there were two in particular that took a toll on me. First, I have had close personal experience and interactions in passing with violent criminals, and their minds and ways of thinking are ugly and burdensome; they are not people you want to make regular friends of. To put these things into words and make people understand was, well, exhausting.

I also found myself quite beaten up after writing each and every violent part. I didn't want the parts to be mild, because the character of Elliot Keller was a horrible, horrible man. It thrilled him to do the things he did to people to the point that the only motivation he had for escaping prison was to have a chance to indulge in his deviant behavior yet once more in his life. Some of the visuals I got, which are what prompt what I write, made me sick, and more than once, I had to step away and breathe.

Now, let's talk about Keller a bit better. Initially, I wrote his character with little to no explanation as to why he was the killer that he was. It didn't matter at first; to me, he was just a bad man, an animal. Many murderers never suffer wrong at the hands of another, yet they choose to harm others over and over, for no other reason than they like it and it's fun.

I changed this. The reason I began to explain a bit about what made Elliot what he was is simple: I had to show readers the ripple effect, that can literally last for centuries, when this type of violence is bestowed by one on another. What happened to Keller, Keller did to others, and it would not stop there... it would never stop. I didn't go into his past to provoke pity or compassion. He is nothing more than a rabid animal, and his actions clearly demonstrate that. With that being said, by the end of the book, you will understand what I mean, and you will still hate him all the more.

Thompson Trails, Virginia is yet another fictional town full of ignorant, innocent unawares that have no idea what is about to hit them. I love to develop these little burgs, and I enjoy creating the people who live blissfully within their boundaries. I grow to love many of the characters, no matter how brief their appearances; as readers know, authors kill people off, no matter their age or how good of a person they are. This happens a lot in Thompson Trails, and I grieved each death. But in reality, killers don't flip coins, and they don't pick and choose. Bad things happen, and they always seem to happen to good people.

Finally, I would like to touch base briefly on Rick and Donna Welk, the owners of the cabin resort, but mostly I want to focus on Donna. Donna and Rick have suffered the loss of a pregnancy, which spurred them to move and buy the cabins. On the outside, Donna is soft, kind, generous, a good wife, and wouldn't hurt a fly. She is hurting that she cannot have a child, and she is simply trying to build a new, happy life around this reality. I believe that readers are going to be surprised by the fiber this little woman is made of, and I think they will be furious at the outcome Keller causes her and the man she loves.

For those of you who are lovers of horror, well, here you go. I hope you enjoy it. I also hope it makes you as sick as it makes me, because it is that horror and sickness that makes us face the harsh realities of life and keeps us on our toes. I didn't write this and then roll it in sugar because it isn't candy; it is a jagged little pill that will slice your throat straight open if you swallow too fast. Believe me, when I say, it is not for children. Best to give fair warning; I wrote this in a manner that it would leave some kind of mark. Hopefully, the mark is a good one.

So, sit down with the lights on and enjoy the terror that is Elliot Keller in 'Passing Through'.

BROTHER'S KEEPER

ISBN-13: 978-1948312134 ISBN-10: 1948312131
ISBN-13: 978-0692744741 ISBN-10: 0692744746
ISBN-13: 978-1948312141 ISBN-10: 194831214X

Psychological Thriller

'Brother's Keeper' is my first psychological thriller, and it was simultaneously fun and difficult to write. It tells the story of Scott Sharp, a widowed traveler whose train makes a stop at the tiny town of Burdensville. Here, Scott tries to assist a waitress being harassed by a drunk and gets himself arrested, which results in pulling the stranger into the dark secrets the town holds, and the secrets won't let him go.

Writing this story was fun for a variety of reasons. It was off the beaten path compared to most books I write. The monster in this book is not a vampire, witch, or zombie; instead, the monster is an unknown man who is murdering women at night who pass through the town. Developing the character of the murderer was a good time; I wanted him to be dull, but intelligent; he needed to be needy, but in control in ways no one understood. He needed to have deep-seated issues that were in such a terrible knot that even those who might care about him didn't know how to sort them out.

Scott walks into Burdensville without the slightest idea what has been happening to this town. He is, utterly and completely, an innocent victim. When he first gets to the café and tries to protect the waitress from the town drunk, he is put under arrest by the sheriff, which is really the first sign that something is off in that town; even the other patrons in the restaurant keep their mouths closed when he implores them to tell the sheriff that he did nothing wrong. The whole place is off, and he can't seem to put his finger on what is happening around him. All Scott knows is that he's trapped in a jail cell waiting to see a judge that won't come for more than a week, but it is there that Scott himself will begin to unravel the goings-on in Burdensville for himself.

Of course, we cannot have a murder mystery without romance, even if it is slight. In the case of Brother's Keeper, I created a slow but sure relationship between Scott and the waitress he tried to save when he was arrested. In the beginning, she was aloof with him, but soon she is forced to take meals to the jail to feed Scott, and it is during this time the two get to know each other. Inevitably, they fall in love, but not before the killer puts her own sanity to the test.

Sheriff Robert Darby is keeping the most secrets in this town, as readers will discover. I chose the sheriff for this role because none of what happens in the book would be possible without the authority that his badge permits him to have. Now, some may say that the storyline in regard to him is somewhat flaky or unrealistic. I would have to tell those readers that this is fiction. The beauty of fiction is exactly what I did in the case of Sheriff Darby and his unutterable secrets.

I tried to put a bit of everything in this book: Old lady hen twins who are the gossipers of the town; Dickie, the café owner, who has great fatherly affection for Denise, and who has seen some of the craziness Burdensville truly has to offer. The town drunk, who is also mentally challenged and basically faces life alone except for the help of the sheriff; he is essential to the novel, in all of its insanity and desperation.

To put things in a nutshell for my readers, there is a past history that the sheriff is actively covering up; he is doing this for more reasons than I can explain here, but his secrets are vile, shameful, and have instilled a sense of obligation in Sheriff Darby that he can never silence. It is, quite literally, a huge burden for him, but he carries these things, and acts upon them, out of the best interest of the townsfolk as a whole, not to mention himself. Readers may feel like Sheriff Darby is something of a bad guy, but I cannot express enough that the things he does which seem so wrong are committed out of a pure heart, a heart that is trying to make things right in a situation where they will never, ever be right again. He is not the guy to hate here, though throughout the pages it clearly seems that way. The reality is, Sheriff Darby is as much of a victim as all of those who have been murdered on the outskirts of the town.

I wanted people to really be in Burdensville while they read this. I also wanted readers to get a very specific feel for the town; Mayberry without a shower. I did my best to convey the gloom of the constant shadows that seem to hang over the place, even when the sun was shining. I also wanted to make it clear that Sheriff Darby wasn't the only one feeling obligation; the entire town does. That's more or less what happens in small-town life and, evil or not, Burdensville is no different.

BLOOD FEATHER AWAKENS

ISBN-10: 0692734082 ISBN-13: 978-0692734087

Crime Thriller

Of all the books I have penned, 'Blood Feather Awakens' was one of the most fun for me. It tells the story of Sam Daniels, a wildlife photographer who, while on assignment in the Amazon jungle, encounters a breathtakingly beautiful but horribly deadly, prehistoric bird. Sam witnesses the bloody killing of his guide but manages to snap a couple of grainy photographs, which he takes to an ornithologist at the University of Washington for identification. That is just the beginning of the tale; Sam and the beautiful Dr. Kate Beck, accompanied by three guides and tailed by a couple of fame-seeking paleontologists, venture back to the jungle to find, and hopefully capture, the murderous creature.

Why was this book so much fun to write? I would have to attribute it simply to the imagination involved in it. From Sam's first encounter with the bird, all the way to its capture and return to the States, I found it was a subject I could really do anything with, if I so chose. I wanted to make the time in the jungle both horrifying, thanks to the evasive bird, and romantic, due to the blossoming romance between Kate and Sam. I also wanted it to be bloody, because let's face it: If a massive prehistoric bird were to attack, well, it would be nothing but bloody.

I also thrived on creating realistic relationships between all of the people. For instance, even though Sam and Kate are in the company of jungle guides, all of them are in this terrible situation together. It was imperative that they talk and laugh, that they come to trust and depend on each other in a way that simply would not take place on a normal jungle tour. Everyone is frightened, but they are also eager. The tour guides are also angry that one of their own has been killed, and they want the threat removed before anyone else is harmed. Sam and Kate want the bird captured and studied; they want to keep it safe while ensuring the safety of the world.

But then we have the two paleontologists, Dr. Harold Kreiger and Dr. Roy Hastings. These two men work at the University of Washington, just as Kate does. Since they are colleagues of hers, she takes Sam to see them when he brings her the photograph of the bird and recognizes it as 'prehistoric' in nature. But, just as she fears, these two begin to see how beating Kate and Sam to the punch will make them famous, and these two men try to get to the creature and locate it before Sam and Kate. This turns out bad for Kreiger and Hastings, but I have to admit, it was more than a pleasure to create the demise these two selfish men deserved.

I wanted the truth about how dangerous this thing was in my own mind to be clearly conveyed; this bird can think, reason, and use logic. The humans which pursue it may outsmart it and capture it, but all it needs is a little time to sort things out and find a way to appease its own bloodthirsty nature. This thing was never meant to be captured; after all, it survived a meteor hitting the Earth millions of years ago, and it has managed to continue its species for the sole reason that 'life will find a way'. The determination that was shown to simply survive needed to clearly reflect its ability to destroy, as well. I believe that I portrayed all of this clearly and concisely, especially at the very end.

So, what is 'Blood Feather'? To put it simply, the creature is, indeed, a bird, but it is prehistoric, related to the 'archaeopteryx' but much larger. In my mind, when humans discover the bones of prehistoric animals, all we really can do is guess as to what their real appearance would have been like. Now, perhaps they did look like that, but I venture to say that it is likely we are off a bit in our assumptions. I did nothing more than to create my own creature, in my own mind. Some of its physical traits are the same, some are different. This is the reason Kate and the paleontologists are uncertain of what it is: They are stuck with an assumed picture in their overly-educated minds.

But exactly what Blood Feather is, is not important. The bottom line is that it's a killer. It lives on flesh and blood, and it gets pleasure from the hunt and chase. It is airborne, so there really is no escape, and it has the ability to somewhat hypnotize its prey with its eerily human eyes. It is meant to confuse and terrify, which is precisely what I designed it for. Its beauty is deceptive; it will lure you in and then end your life. To be honest, this was the most fun for me: Writing about presumptuous humans who are scrambling around out of their element, trying to get the best of nature's perfect killing machine.

I truly hope readers are as entertained by this story as I was by writing it. I tried to keep it light and simple without compromising fear or blood. I also wanted to tell a story that would keep the reader turning pages. I think that those who read this fun and frightening story will appreciate it in the end, for what I intended it to be.

SHATTERED DREAMS

ISBN-10: 0997876719 ISBN-13: 978-0997876710

Crime Thriller

When I sat down to write 'Shattered Dreams', I did it with one purpose in mind, and it was a very simple purpose: To tell a story. It isn't like my other novels in that it is in no way 'supernatural' or 'psychological'; it is just the tale of a man with dreams who brought them to life, only to have them ripped away from him in the most desperate and unfair way possible. It is something that could really happen; there are no zombies or vampires, and there are no magical formulas being produced. Only a man, his dream, and the enemy who hates him.

So, let me begin with my main character, Jimmy O'Brien. Jimmy is a good boy from the beginning, the offspring of a loser Irish father and devoted Italian mother. From as far back as Jimmy can remember, he has had a single dream: To be a cop, and to fight the bad guys. He makes all the right choices, even from youth, to obtain his goal; he even goes the extra mile on more than one occasion.

Let's begin at the start, or as close to it as effectively possible. Jimmy's mother raises him alone, thanks to his father running off with another. The man had it all at one point: A wife, a son, and a good job. But rather than acting according to his priorities, he not only cheats and leaves, but he also resorts to criminal behavior that includes beating up the woman he left his wife for. Jimmy despises this behavior, even going so far as to refuse to call his father 'dad'. Along with television cop shows, it is this behavior that dictates Jimmy's hatred toward those who harm others in any criminal way.

But in his mother, Jimmy has a person who would go to the ends of the Earth for her son to be happy and well provided for. She supports him in all of his ventures, and even though she is afraid for his safety, she also backs him in his pursuit of a police career. Luciana O'Brien is a wonderful, moral woman who deserves to have something good happen to her in her life.

Jimmy has several other people who support him, from friends to the chief of his hometown police department, Matias Garcia. Over the years, all the right doors open at the right times, and Jimmy, true to his form, always walks straight through each and every one of them. Soon, he is a grown man with a job working as a real police officer, and he is nearing his goal of becoming chief for the entire department. He has a beautiful fiancé, and everything is coming together just as he had always planned.

But when an old school rival of Jimmy's comes back into the picture as a runner for the Mexican cartel, things take a terrible turn. All of his dreams are now being threatened, and before he knows it, corruption in the department is plotting to steal the dreams he has held so dear to his heart, taking everything and everyone he loves as well.

What is the point of this book? As the writer, I would have to firmly say that the point is: Nothing ever goes as planned, and more often than not, our hearts are broken terribly. Jimmy is innocent, quite literally, in this story, but by the end of the book, he is suffering consequences which only the evil should have to endure. Why? Because, to put it as simply as possible, that's life.

The things which happen to Jimmy at the hands of others are much less impactful if the reader doesn't have a firm grasp on who this young man is, morally speaking. This is someone who would rather die than do harm to another. This is someone who really couldn't tell a lie if he wanted to. Jimmy is trustworthy, soft-hearted, compassionate, and bent on doing the right thing. His every action is motivated by a solid desire to operate out of integrity, and nothing else.

All of his hardship towards the end stems from a toxic friendship he had in the first grade with a boy named Kevin Marshall. Kevin is a bad seed, through and through. When the boy gets caught for stealing from a classmate, Jimmy knows, without a doubt, that he cannot continue their friendship. But it is Kevin Marshall who Jimmy must confront in high school for dealing drugs, and it is Kevin Marshall who sparks the chain of events in adulthood which ultimately prove to be Jimmy's destruction. The point? The past will come back to haunt you, even if you weren't the one doing the haunting in the first place.

As far as Jimmy is concerned, he is a character that I have a certain amount of love for, in a literal way. I admire the man I created, and as I created his life and heartaches, I hurt for him. I found myself infuriated with the bad guys I put in his life, but at the same time, I realized I wasn't willing to bail him out of his injustices. This is the life I created for Henry James O'Brien, and this is his destiny, unfortunately.

I think readers will like this book, but not because it is frightening or abstract. Readers will enjoy it because of the level of reality they will find in its pages. I also think they will feel the same way about Jimmy that I do, and I believe they will experience anger at the unfairness that goes on in his life. In the end, 'Shattered Dreams' is a highly relatable story for anyone who decides to venture into its pages.

REQUIEM FOR THE CAGED

ISBN-10: 1948312026 ISBN-13: 978-1948312028

Romantic Suspense

Coming from the perspective of someone who creates, I believe I can say with confidence that my new book, 'Requiem for the Caged', may not be for everyone. I knew this from the start, and even as I sat down to write it, I simply wanted to tell a story I hadn't told before, and it happened to fall into a far different category than my fans are used to.

First of all, this particular story has nothing to do with the undead, or bloodsuckers of any kind. It has nothing to do with aliens, or youth potions, or tainted futuristic seas. It is a love story, pure and simple. Unconventional? Of course. But love is never really conventional in any way, now is it? So, why should it be conventional in the pages of a book?

First, I would like to begin by discussing the premise. Jason Brandtley is a good young man. He has just returned from being a prisoner of war overseas and is facing the impending death of his mother. He is a young man with a gentle spirit and full of integrity, but he has suffered many recent traumas, and with his mother being sick, they really aren't over yet. But that doesn't change the fact that his heart and soul are clean, and the motives of his heart are always based on his desire to do the right thing and help.

After his mother dies, Jason inherits the family sheep ranch, but he is having to run operations on his own. Lonely and depressed, Jason longs for a wife to share his life with. He is eager, and he is willing to do what it takes to find a good woman to walk by his side.

Andrea is a waitress who lives and works in Cheyenne, about thirty minutes away. He meets her while having lunch in the park one day, and Jason is stricken with her immediately. But Andrea is a polar opposite to Jason, as readers will see. Unlike Jason, a much-loved only child, Andrea comes from a family that is harsh and uncaring; her mother has essentially turned her back on the girl, forcing her to be strong and emotionally detached when it comes to life. The pair does have one thing in common, however: they both have suffered heartbreak several times at the hands of love interests. The thing that sets them apart is how they have chosen to respond to the pain. While Jason is able to somewhat put it behind him, Andrea's every action and reaction is based on the abuse she has suffered from men.

Jason doesn't know this, and he begins to pursue her, only to be shot down in flames and actually assaulted by her ex for his efforts. This assault sends the ex-POW over the edge, and he determines to teach Andrea a lesson. He builds a cage in his basement for her, abducts her, and refuses her release until she changes her ways.

That is as strange as this novel gets, however. It is here that the two, who are now in each other's constant company, begin to get to know one another. They begin to realize that everyone suffers heartache, but it is never a reason to re-inflict. They also begin to see each other differently in this light, and inevitably, love begins to grow.

Now, there is no torture or murder involved in this novel. The desire of Jason's heart is to genuinely help Andrea, even though he has gone to a terrifying and unacceptable length to do so. Andrea is only initially frightened of harm; she is soon convinced he couldn't hurt her if he wanted to, and this realization is the turning point in their relationship.

Why did I decide to write such a story, especially when most of my works are thrillers? Well, I would have to say that, in my opinion and from my experience, love can be the strangest and scariest thing of all. I wanted to try romantic suspense and see how two people from totally different backgrounds react to each other's pain. I wanted to play with the idea that, even if someone 'flips their lid', so to speak, they can still love and be loved. I also wanted to express the deep importance of communication in learning to love and accept one another for all that each of us is. This involves understanding that each of us is made up of all of our happiness and heartaches. Each laugh and every tear are what we consist of. Most of the time, these things can cause us to act in a manner that is repulsive or frightening, or painful, to those around us, just like in the cases of both Jason and Andrea. But these things can also be overcome if the other is willing to look at the whole person instead of just the ugly parts. That is where the beauty of love comes in.

Yes, Dear Readers, this is what you may label a 'romance' or 'love story', and that may be a jagged pill for some of you to swallow coming from me. But the fact is, love is just as much a part of life as our fear of the monster in the closet, or the stalker outside the window. It is even more a part of life than any of these because it is the basis for our sanity and survival.

It is my sincere hope that you all enjoy this book for what it is: A simple, yet complicated, tale of two people who find love in the most unlikely of places. It is the story about cages, and how all of us live in them in one way or another. Most of all, it is about acceptance of the person trapped in the cage across from yours.

OUT TO SEA

ISBN-10: 099787676X ISBN-13: 978-0997876765

Romantic Suspense

'Out to Sea' was a project that I had to walk a fine line with. I intended for it to be a work with a very pertinent message, while forming a bond between star-crossed teen lovers that is destined to end with the cruise they were on. With the state of the future world in shambles, it was somewhat difficult to know when and where romance was truly appropriate; after all, the planet is dying before the eyes of the main characters, and they are literally watching everyone basically celebrate it. It's the sort of thing that can ruin the mood.

The basic plot of the book revolves around a chemical spill which has made all the water on Earth poisonous, even to the touch. Man has created an electrolyte-based alternative for drinking, and other methods which are less than natural are used for bathing, swimming, etc. The fact of the matter is that the end will come as a direct result of this, and most everyone is painfully aware that the future is dark and grim.

There are those, however, who have found a way to exploit the situation. The spill has made the appearance of the water indescribably gorgeous, even entrancing, to a certain level. People purchase atrociously priced luxury cruises for the sole purpose of gawking at the lifeless seas, and they seem to have no care for what the façade of beauty they are looking at really means. It is truly a horrible thing, and I wanted the level of depravity and complacency to which human beings stoop to be stark and ugly.

Tripp Young is my main character on this ocean voyage. As the only son of wealthy parents, he is expected to go on these yearly excursions with them. They are two of the countless who have bought into the horrible exploitation of the planet's impending death, and they seem blind to the reality of it all. To them, and all others like them, it is an amusement park ride, of sorts.

But Tripp is neither ignorant nor calloused to what is taking place. He looks at his existence as taking place in two categories: Before the Spill, and After the Spill, and the planets in both are very different places indeed. For a seventeen-year-old, he is very in touch with logic and sense, as well as the brokenhearted emotion he nurses for the world that was once lush with grass and other plant life; a world where you could jump in a river and swim. Tripp had to be angry, but I also knew it had to be a righteous, self-controlled anger, an anger with a purpose.

While on this joke of a cruise, Tripp meets Heidi Collins, and is instantly smitten with the smart, petite environmentally conscious redhead. Never having a real girlfriend before, he easily becomes consumed with spending as much time together while on the water as they can, and her feelings are the same. Together, they witness some pretty horrific things, which can all be attributed to the tainted sea that surrounds them. It pulls them closer and closer as the days pass.

One such scene involves a child who goes missing during the cruise. The ship's staff searches high and low for her, to no avail. Tripp, Heidi, and two of their friends watch and listen in disgusted awe as the ship continues on the water, because the show must go on. Finally, the kids decide to look for the girl themselves, on the sly.

This is one tragedy that takes place aboard the ship. It was important to convey the state of mind of those who enjoyed what the spill had done; depraved indifference and selfishness filled their souls. I contemplated the accomplishment, though it may have seemed overly dramatic in manner, at times.

As for Tripp and Heidi's love, it was doomed from the start; in my mind, this was to be a sad tale of not only the results of man's wreaking havoc on Mother Earth, but of unrequited love. These two kids genuinely love each other, and they swear to be together again. Deep inside, they both know they will not, but it is something they are not willing to even consider. I wanted the reader to feel the hopelessness and emptiness they felt at the thought of the day they would say goodbye, and I truly hope I managed to get that done. I wanted their interactions to be intensely emotional and painful, so they could be tangible to the person with the book.

To put it simply, 'Out to Sea' is an environmentally conscious romantic suspense that has no blissful ending, but it tells a story, and it teaches a lesson. It may not feel good, but lessons rarely do. I think by the end of this book, whether the reader loves it or hates it, they will never forget it. I wrote it to be the kind of story that sticks, even if it isn't popular for the particular content or level of fiction. With that being said, this is one of my personal favorites as a writer, and it had an impact on me that my other works haven't. It may be a fiction novel, but the pain and despair I put in the pages was anything but a fairy tale; I'm confident the emotion will help get the message across loud and clear.

PASSAGE OF TIME

ISBN-10: 0997876727 ISBN-13: 978-0997876727

Romantic Suspense

'Passage of Time' is actually one of my personal favorites, and I hope you enjoy reading it as much as I enjoyed writing it.

This was never intended to be a thriller novel; it just barely makes it into the science fiction realm, only doing so because of the 'fountain of youth' premise. Mostly, this book is a romantic suspense, but it is also a story of time wasted in an effort to live forever. It is a tale which has been shaped by years of regret and sadness, which are only realized at the very end.

Calvin Cooper is a man with a mission. A scientist, both by trade and by nature, Calvin wants to help others look and feel younger. Early on, he meets Elaina, the woman destined to be the love of his life and his eternal companion. Together, Calvin believes they will conquer the world. With her patience, he will come up with the end-all, be-all solution, and then they will be together forever, literally.

There is no end to Elaina's loyalty or patience. It was important to create in her, a character who is totally devoted, no matter what she may face with her man. Throughout their lives, and his work, she is his rock, and his love for her knows no bounds. Unfortunately, she is also the only one who looks at things realistically, and Calvin is destined to learn one of the most painful lessons of his life through her: People were never meant to live forever.

One situation the two endure together involves an animal rights activist group who has targeted Calvin, believing that his work involves harming animals. But even through this scary incident in their lives, Elaina is his strong tower and primary support, and his love for her grows.

Over time, Calvin begins to make progress with his formula, and while his wife is extremely supportive when it comes to meeting his goals, she is not one who believes that human beings should endure indefinitely. But she is the kind of woman who will ignore her own beliefs if it means backing up the man she loves. Calvin, however, is oblivious to all of this. The years pass, and more progress is made. As he considers all the time he has spent focusing on his work, he tries to push the guilt aside that he feels for putting poor Elaina on the back burner. He reassures himself that when the formula is perfected, the two of them will enjoy eternity in each other's arms.

Ralph Gordon is another character who was necessary to the lesson Calvin is set to learn. Ralph comes on as Calvin's assistant, and they too end up forging an unbreakable friendship. He, like Elaina, is dedicated, and he truly cares about the person who is doing all the work. But Ralph just wants to live his days out in peace; living forever isn't even remotely attractive to him. Calvin seems to be stuck in a huge lack of understanding; both Ralph and Elaina could spell things out for him, but his genius has stolen his ability to look at things from the heart. Without Ralph, Calvin would likely just consider that Elaina's opinions are formed because she is something of an emotional woman.

Another character who tries to get the point across, in a much more subdued manner, is Noah Carter, the sick old man who first owned Maddie, the horse. But when given the option to continue on, permanently, in his newfound youth, Noah gratefully refuses, explaining his stance clearly and concisely. This is yet another example of Calvin being so blinded by his dreams that he has become numb to life's realities; he has no grasp whatsoever on why these people would refuse, nor is he able to consider giving up.

Calvin Cooper is, in a sense, every man. Anyone with any level of personal accountability or love in their heart wants to give the world to those who are the objects of his affection. If that man is able to cause his wife to live forever, he would, as would Calvin. But Calvin has lost touch with the very things that make us all human, and in his effort to work literal miracles, he allows his entire life to pass him by. It isn't until he comes to the point of being surrounded in his success while in utter isolation that Calvin begins to understand what he gave up for a dream that was never meant to become a reality.

Yes, I wrote 'Passage of Time' to be a love story. I wrote it with the intent of making readers feel the love between Calvin and Elaina in a very tangible sense, and I hope I succeeded in that goal. But above and beyond that, this book was meant to make the reader consider who they have to love, and whether or not they are doing all that they can to demonstrate that love during the limited time they have. As we all know, there is no secret potion, no 'ElainaYouth' to consume that will give us countless years to revel in the gift of life. What each of us has, all that we have, is the here and now that ultimately makes up that thing we call 'today'.

So, in consideration of the above, I believe that mature readers will find 'Passage of Time' to be compelling and thought-provoking. I believe it will stimulate a spirit of gratefulness, when allowed, and I also believe it will leave readers with the simple satisfaction of having read a good book. In the end, that is the purpose of fiction, after all, and 'Passage of Time' is no exception.

DEAD ON THE WATER

ISBN-10: 0997876700 ISBN-13: 978-0997876703
ISBN-10: 1948312905 ISBN-13: 978-1948312905
ISBN-10: 1948312921 ISBN-13: 978-1948312929
ISBN-10: 194831293X ISBN-13: 978-1948312936

Zombie Thriller

This is another zombie contribution which I put a bit of a spin on. 'Dead on the Water' chronicles the story of a Fantasy Lines cruise ship which has a passenger who got bit by a dog during a shopping spree with her parents in Belize. Not knowing that the dog is carrying a terrible, zombie-making virus, the bite-victim re-boards the ship, and it returns to the vast ocean. Soon, the entire vessel is overrun with zombies, and those who have not been infected are fighting for their lives in the middle of the sea.

The first thing I would like to say about this particular book is that I allowed the zombies to be able to think, speak, and function, but they are the undead, nevertheless. The leader of the zombie pack, Captain James McElroy, even continues to be the leader in death that he was in life, and his plan is to not only take over the entire ship, but to get to land and carry on spreading the vile sickness when they dock in Houston.

This is a fast-paced book; once the action starts, it is pretty much non-stop. Being on a cruise ship, those who are still normal have very limited resources or means of escape. The ship has approximately three-thousand zombies trying to get to the last remaining survivors, so most of the ship's staff that are still alive are essentially barricaded into one part of the ship or another, including the bridge and a fitness center. They are desperate, with no weapons and no way to get off the ship without guaranteeing their own demise.

While it is about zombies, and there are several very graphic scenes, I do not believe it is necessarily a scary book. I tried to use dialogue in a surreal manner, especially coming from the monsters, in an effort to show the craziness and terrifying truth about the situation, but I didn't want it to be too heavy. My vision was simply to relate the hopelessness of the situation without making the book burdensome to read; I wanted it to be on the 'lighter' side, if possible.

Now, I presented a couple of different situations in the book. The primary one takes place on the ship; the second is happening at a shady lab in Belize, where the girl was bitten by a dog in the alley. This lab is sort of an underground operation run by a somewhat 'mad' scientist and his assistant, Bruce Ward; the good doctor relocated after the States stopped his experimentation. The long and short of it is that this lab has gone haywire, and its infected rats are beginning to run rampant. The CDC tries to gain control of this situation, which is sort of a side-line story to give you, the reader, a bit of hope that this craziness will be contained. I should warn you, especially my new readers: Don't get your hopes up. I find it difficult to imagine happy endings when it comes to the genres I write in, and I find it much easier to be horribly realistic. But let's face it, I write about completely unrealistic stuff. What I'm trying to say is, the glory of fiction is in its falseness, but the impact of fiction is found in its painful reality. If a zombie apocalypse really happened, would the ending really be a good one? I think not; it would be hopeless and desperate, and that is the painful reality of this book.

Speaking of hope, let's talk about George Meade, Captain McElroy's assistant. So, we have the CDC battling things on land, but those still living on the ship are literally fighting a losing battle; they are fish in a barrel. If the zombies reach land, there will be a literal outbreak, and nothing the CDC is doing in Belize will matter. I allow George to escape in a lifeboat because someone on that damn cruise ship has to be smart enough to get away and get help. Pretty daunting task, don't you think? To reach the docking point before the ship, baking in the sun with no water, and having been through a terribly traumatic and unbelievable experience? Well, all I have to say about his success or failure is, you'll just have to see.

On another topic, I didn't get too deep with any of the characters as far as their personal appearance or personalities. There are many characters in 'Dead on the Water'; only a few hold the limelight, and none for very long; ultimately, it is 'every man for himself'.

So, as far as my second zombie tale goes, I hope you enjoy it. It's a little lighter than you might expect, but it is fast-paced, and you'll find plenty of gruesome scenes. 'Dead on the Water' is an easy and entertaining read. I hope you'll check out this book, and have fun reading it, too!

PERMANENT INK

ISBN-10: 0997876735 ISBN-13: 978-0997876734

Zombie Thriller

I wrote 'Permanent Ink' with mostly one message to convey: The price of greed can be astronomical, and most often, it is horribly destructive.

This is the story of a stationers' company that is on the brink of bankruptcy, but they have an ace in the hole: A new ink that appears almost holographic once it is on paper. Knowing that the kids will love it, Aspen Stationers' pushes for quick release of the pens developed to dispense the ink, wanting it available for public purchase before the school year starts. But the executives at Aspen have a secret: In the lab, the ink has had an adverse effect on rats, causing them to attack each other to the death, then bringing them back to life more violent and bloodthirsty than ever. Because this only happens when the ink is still wet, Aspen has convinced themselves that the world will be safe, and consumers will be none the wiser.

In an effort to show how widespread the destruction is, I scattered the storyline around a bit: One particular incident involving the ink takes place in a hospital in Thornton, Colorado. Another, in Aspen, where the company is located, and finally Monte Vista. The outbreak is taking place in the suburbs, but the local government is trying to figure things out, and has even called in the CDC. The catastrophe has even reached other areas, but for the sake of the story, I have kept the text limited to areas in Colorado.

First, let's look at the outbreak at the hospital. When a young girl gets the ink in a scrape, she is soon terribly ill. Her mother rushes her to the hospital to be seen, and the child is admitted. Even though she is exhibiting strange, and even violent, behavior, her mother is driven to comfort her, which leads to an attack. Before anyone even understands what is taking place, the 'zombie' sickness has spread like wildfire, and both patients and employees of the health care center are forced to fight for their lives. A pair of physicians are beginning to figure things out, slowly but surely, but will they solve the problem before it's too late?

The hospital scenes are fast-paced; it is chaos there, and the panic the characters are feeling should be tangible. I did the best I could to convey this, without giving too much hope to the situation, because frankly, I felt the situation in Thornton was fairly close to being hopeless.

In the situation with Aspen Stationers' scientist, Randy Carstens, he is fully aware of the potential for disaster, and he is sickened by the complacency of the executives in charge. Randy manages to get himself fired, but that doesn't keep him from returning and trying to stop the ball, which has already been set rolling. While there, the company's CEO, Roger McGinley, falls victim to the zombie rats while trying to force Randy to comply at gunpoint. Fortunately, Randy is able to escape and notify Aspen Police, but by the time they understand what is happening, they have a pretty big mess on their hands.

Which takes us to Brian Olson, a soon-to-be ninth grader at Monte Vista High School. Brian's single mother couldn't afford to buy him the expensive pen, but his best friend Caleb comes through. Brian tests the ink, which is said to smudge easily, with a finger. Unfortunately, he has a papercut, and the ink gets into his bloodstream. Overnight, the boy has died and becomes one of the bloodthirsty undead; his poor, unsuspecting mother is his first victim. Soon, the town is pretty much on lockdown, and the petrified people of Monte Vista are waiting for the CDC to come and save the day.

'Permanent Ink' is a zombie story, plain and simple, filled with the flesh-eating monsters that are all the rage at the current time. It is meant to gross readers out, to a certain extent, but mostly, with all of the chaotic scenes aside, I wanted to really convey a message. Corporate greed is the catalyst behind this horrible outbreak, wreaking havoc on unsuspecting consumers who have been blindsided by their timely marketing tactics. The worst part is, Aspen Stationers' is more than suspicious of the potential for damage that the ink has; they know full well what it can do, and they just don't care. This type of manipulation takes place every day in our world, with results just as destructive, only slower and less obvious. This truth is really what is behind the message in this book.

Of course, things have to be cleared up, and solutions must be found so life can go on. But as I mentioned earlier, I neither saw nor felt any positive resolution to this particular story, and as a writer, I had to struggle to make a way for the sun to rise on these towns again, with hope. I firmly believe that, if this were a true story, there would be no one left to write about it; the world would be taken out systematically by the undead, which Aspen Stationers' created when they released Lumiosa ink to the public.

It is my hope that readers are able to enjoy this book for what it truly is: A work of fiction that provides yet another take on zombies and how they might come to be walking, and terrorizing, among us. It is meant for entertainment, but I think the moral behind this made-up tale makes it possible to consider other possibilities, and hopefully, it causes readers to think about the items they are willingly choosing to consume.

LIVING LEGACY

ISBN-10: 0692517243 ISBN-13: 978-0692517246

Zombie Thriller

'Living Legacy: Among the Dead' is the first complete book I wrote. Though it is a very quick read, I believe readers will get just as much out of its pages as they would if it were a larger novel. Mostly, it was written for the sake of the love story which I have woven into the apocalyptic situation.

Alicia Gaden is a biology major at UCLA; she has her goals lined up and her future planned. She is also a very good student and person; she doesn't galivant around with different boys or party. Rather, she remains single, and keeps her primary focus on her studies.

Jace Booth is pretty much the same type of person as Alicia, with the exception being that he majors in chemistry. The pair meet up when everyone starts changing; people become violent, and their skin begins to pale and rot. For some reason, the two of them seem to have avoided drinking the water, allowing them to survive the strange phenomenon taking place, but together they pursue knowledge regarding why this is happening. As it turns out, there are no two better for the job.

The book is told from Alicia's perspective, which is not typical for me. I wanted to convey the zombie outbreak from the female point of view.

Alicia, in the initial pages, is pretty much on her own. Sure, she has a roommate, Lilith, but the girl really doesn't have much of a purpose, except for the sake of the reality of college life. No, Alicia is witnessing the changes in others entirely on her own. She wants to figure out what is happening and why it doesn't seem to be happening to her. She meets Jace during a trip to the UCLA student library, which turns out to be a relief because he seems unaffected as well.

Unbeknownst to the two of them, the problem is in the LA water supply. All-Purpose Plastics has been developing the 'plastic of the future': Soligel. Unfortunately, they push it through for federal approval, and an unaware maintenance man ends up disposing of a chemical spill improperly. He, too, is affected, but corporate executives take matters into their own hands and shut him up for good. It is only through their own tests and dangerous missions that Alicia and Jace are able to figure out that the problem is in the water. Once that is pinpointed, they must come up with a way to solve the outbreak before it is too late.

I wanted the main characters to be highly intelligent, but I also wanted them to be as courageous as possible. Let's face it, and I am sad to say, most college students today would panic and buckle if they found themselves in this situation. If these two are going to survive, and if any love is going to grow between them, it was essential for them to be strong and determined, and to have a mutually beneficial skill set if they wanted to get the job done. These are the main characteristics that were the foundation for Jace Booth and Alicia Gaden.

Now, it is true that I didn't really deal with the executives of All-Purpose Plastics in a manner that would be satisfying. The fact is, to me, they would be succumbing to the outbreak in their own time and manner. That would be their just deserts. In order for the book to have the combined flavors that I gave it, there was no room for justice, at least, not the kind of justice these people rightfully deserved. Greed and malice are sicknesses of the soul; it was best to let karma deal with them and focus on Alicia and Jace.

I added the tidbit regarding Alicia possibly becoming pregnant for a couple of different reasons. First, it would solidify their relationship and drive them on to continue the fight at hand at any cost. I wanted the relationship between the two of them to be held together by more than sex; my intent with these two was a lifelong commitment, even if there was the possibility that life could end at any second. Second, a pregnancy would be representative of life finding a way; this gives the reader a renewed sense of hope, both for the lives of the main characters, and for their success in completing their mission against the zombies and the tainted water.

I also wanted them to be able to conduct their research in a setting that provided them with some level of peace and comfort. This is where the house comes in. It was owned by a zombie victim named Belinda

Smythe, who is caught off guard by the undead monsters. Her car is left there, and has run itself out of gasoline. Finding this location was essential to their success; I mean, let's be real: If a couple of college kids are going to save the day and fall in love while they're at it, having a comfortable base of operations is essential.

Without giving away the ending, I would just like to say that Alicia and Jace are very crafty, and they have more than enough reasons to accomplish their goal to defeat the zombies and fix the issue successfully. But as we all know, a good story never ends without some kind of lure or suggestion about the real state of things. Perhaps Alicia and Jace firmly believe that they have fixed the problem in the water, but did they really? Only time will tell. I sincerely hope that readers enjoy 'Living Legacy: Among the Dead', and appreciate it for the fun piece of fiction it was meant to be.

ZOMBIE DIARIES

Homecoming Junior Year
ISBN-10: 0997876778 ISBN-13: 978-0997876772
Winter Formal Junior Year
ISBN-10: 0997876786 ISBN-13: 978-0997876789
Prom Junior Year
ISBN-10: 0997876794 ISBN-13: 978-0997876796

Girl Zombie

'Zombie Diaries" is a series I have written about the funny, off-beat story of Mavis Harvey, Girl Zombie. In the beginning of this first installment, the main character inadvertently drinks tainted tap water, and as the book progresses, she begins to experience some fairly crazy changes. As the introductory novel to the series, readers will get to know Mavis a bit, and they will get a strong sense of the personality of this girl who is slowly turning into a flesh-eating monster.

This is not a horror novel in the traditional sense, and I never intended it to be. What I wanted to do with Mavis and her life was have fun by asking, 'What would it be like if a normal, everyday girl were to experience this type of change alone, out of the blue? What if she retained her intelligence and logic, realizing something was happening, but not sure what? How would she deal with it?' I wanted the book to be light, with a tad of humor, and I wanted it to contain a story that was acceptable for reading for an audience of most any age.

In the beginning stages of Mavis' journey, she feels a little off but soon finds that her appetite has grown out of control overnight. She is a slight girl, so this gets the attention of her mother, who believes she is ill and takes Mavis to the doctor. Insisting that she feels great, and with no other real symptoms other than insatiable hunger, her physician diagnoses her with anemia, directs her to take iron supplements, and tells her mother to let her eat when she wants for the time being.

Unbeknownst to those in her life, Mavis soon begins to crave more than just an overabundance of food; she wants raw meat, and the bloodier the better. I used raw liver (of any kind) as her 'snack', so to speak, for a couple of different reasons. One: There really isn't a bloodier meat with a grosser texture; it seems to fit as a zombie snack perfectly, and two: Because most everyone hates liver, and the thought of it raw is unbearable. The temptation to gross out my readers was as irresistible to me as raw liver is to Mavis.

As her 'illness' slowly progresses, it begins to come out a bit in gray flaky spots on her skin and prominent dark veins showing through her flesh. She is getting pale, and her mother worries about that fact. Mavis also gains no weight, which is strange, because she is constantly eating one thing or another. Jane Harvey only mentions her concerns in passing, but when she catches her daughter eating a raw pork chop bone, she feels justified in her concerns. Mavis is a loving daughter and has always been trustworthy. Because she feels fine, she is able to tell her mother to not be worried, 'It's just the anemia'; Jane believes her.

I also felt that it was important to make Mavis very likeable; I wanted her to have strong morals and goals. She is very friendly and kindhearted, but she doesn't hang around with a lot of friends. Indeed, she has only one, Kim Coleman, and they have been best friends since the first grade.

She likes boys, but has never been on a date simply because school has been more important, but also because she has never been asked. While she is pretty and slender, she also seemed a bit bookish and nerdy to the opposite sex; she knows it, and it never bothered her before. Kim is a bit heavy, very pretty, and just a tad self-absorbed; she has never dated either, possibly because of her friendship with Mavis.

After Mavis is 'infected', she is asked on her first date ever. A star football player for her high school tells her he has liked her for a long time, and works up the courage to ask her to the homecoming dance. At this point readers may begin to see Mavis as the teenager she is; as she begins to get to know love interest Jeff Deason, her feminine side begins to really show through her words and actions.

Mavis likes him very much, and she is excited about going to the dance with someone other than her best friend. The problem begins, however, when the pair start to date before the big event. She realizes that she can smell him, and he smells delicious, but so do a lot of other people.

With no real worries, she continues to get to know the young man and live her life, but when she dreams of eating a delivery man one day, she vows to never do such a horrible act. She is shocked and dismayed at her own dreams, but not because she killed a man; she is ashamed because she ate him, and that is the only reason. Convinced it is best to keep the dream to herself, Mavis continues with her plans for homecoming night with Jeff.

I didn't intend for ZD1 to be bloody, or scary. What my vision for Mavis consisted of was something laid-back and fun to read, something that takes an already insane idea (zombies) and turns it into a story that takes away the sting of the same old idea. With that in mind, readers of any age will enjoy the story of Mavis, and they will want to stick this crazy experience out with her until the bitter end.

I encourage you to enjoy 'Zombie Diaries' and continue to follow this tongue-in-cheek heroine as she slowly, but surely, comes to terms with what is happening to her.

OVERTAKEN CAPTIVE STATES

ISBN-13: 978-1948312004 ISBN-10: 194831200X
ISBN-13: 978-0692489314 ISBN-10: 0692489312
ISBN-13: 978-1948312127 ISBN-10: 1948312123

Supernatural Thriller

This particular novel was the second book that I have written, and it is the only one I have penned with a focus on alien invasion. I think that the premise of the book is good, and the story is fairly spooky overall.

The prologue consists of nothing but random characters in scattered cities. It relates the very first moments of the invasion of the Oppressors from varying points of view. As far as an introduction goes, it is superficial, but it is effective because of this fact. Once the invasion becomes confirmed reality, I introduce the main characters of the book and tell the story.

This is an invasion story that really doesn't have the obligatory 'happy ending'; nothing about this situation could possibly end happily for humans, and I wasn't going to pretend it could. But to me, the invasion itself is not the scariest part of 'Overtaken'; being tested to determine if you are of enough value to live or die is even more frightening. The pressure of the situation, and the truth that even if you pass the tests, you will go to a foreign planet forever, is a grim thing to have on one's shoulders. In the real world, people would commit suicide if faced with the prospect.

But there always has to be a hero or two, even if they ultimately are only saving themselves. The character of Josh Nichols takes readers to Washington, DC, with front row seats. Josh works as a code writer at the Pentagon. He is a young, ambitious man with all of his supposed ducks in a row. Something of a workaholic, Josh has no family or girlfriend in DC; he was born and raised in Iowa, so he's still fairly green behind the ears.

Kamryn Reynolds is Josh's polar opposite. With a history of crime and street-life, she is a seasoned, semi-tough computer hacker who is always dodging the law. When the invasion takes place, these two meet accidentally, and soon Josh is working side-by-side with her for the president himself. Together, they search for a weak spot in the computer system that is running all of the alien spacecrafts. Their plan is to hack into it and let down protective shields, making the Oppressors open to human attack.

In an effort to pick up the pace, I gave humankind a deadline, so to speak. In large numbers, people are led to testing facilities, separated from their families and never to be seen again. These groups are done by sections throughout each included city. Josh and Kamryn must get this all figured out before they are herded away for themselves.

What is the testing for? This was the fun part for me, because the concept does spark fear in my heart. So, am I being tested for strengths, or weaknesses?

What will be done to me, extermination-wise, if I fail either way? Worse yet, what will happen to me if I 'pass'? It all consists of question marks which dance gleefully around the unknown, and the unknown is the scariest thing in the world.

Now, we should probably consider the question: With all of the resources and skills at the fingertips of the United States government, especially when it comes to employees, why choose Josh and Kamryn to try and save the day? Well, dear reader, I think the answer is obvious: It makes for a story that is much more fun and relatable. But seriously, isn't it hard to relate to every super-hero character there is? Real life consists of real people, and that's what these two kids represent.

'Superior' is another character I enjoyed playing with. He is the soulless, alien leader of the Oppressors, and his mission is destruction to his gain. He couldn't care less about these 'humans'. To him, they are like cockroaches in a deserted house; they must be exterminated before the new tenants can move in. From that perspective, it is his nature to be who he is and do what he is doing to humanity, just as it is our nature to love puppies and kitties and show compassion. The Oppressors are not able to think or feel in the same way.

The president, and all of his high-end, star-spangled advisors, are at a loss. The reason for this is simple: If aliens came, and they had the technology to get here, chances are they have it over on us. It would be a losing battle if indeed we had to fight one. None of their computer geniuses think like Kamryn or Josh, which forces the president's hand. I almost wrote these high-rankers as 'bumbling', because that's how I saw them in my mind's eye. They have been so busy thinking they were omnipotent that they never stopped to think about their own mortality. Bumbling, like I said.

Then we have the end. Yes, there are survivors; the Oppressors promised there would be. But there are more victims than escapees; the planet is virtually demolished. Not to mention the people who didn't pass and were killed, or worse yet, the ones stranded on the blazing, crumbling planet. I feel safe when I say there are no winners here, but there wouldn't be if this ever really happened, either.

I liked the way all of the 'hows' and 'whys' worked out the way they did. I hope readers have a good time with this grim story, and I hope that they get out of it all I put into it: From the fiction to the fear.

LUCIFER'S ANGEL

ISBN-10: 0692733280 ISBN-13: 978-0692733288

Supernatural Thriller

'Lucifer's Angel' is a book which tells the tale of a young girl raised in a very religious home, who experiences a year of terrible loss. The result of these painful occurrences is loss of the faith she has had her entire life, and in an effort to find a 'god' she can trust, the young teen turns to witchcraft. Unfortunately, she has no idea what she is getting herself into, and the consequences of her choice to revert are devastating.

Sarah Hathaway is your average teenager. She has lived in the fictional town of Paradise, her entire life, the only child of her parents, and their pride and joy. She has a very normal, happy life: Sarah has her best friend, Michelle, and her beloved border collie, Mitzi. She also has an uncommonly close relationship with her grandmother, church pianist Emma Holt. Everything in her life is perfect, and she is completely unprepared for the series of tragedies that take place.

For me, the best thing about writing 'Lucifer's Angel' was the freedom I had to add as many twists and surprises as I saw fit. This is an unpredictable book, and I like it that way. Even to the very last pages, when you finally think you have what is happening to Sarah figured out, I switch it up. But what I have to say is that the nature of this book is the perfect breeding ground for such surprise, and without it, this would not have come anywhere near making the point I intended it to make.

So, then, what is the point? Well, I could say there are a few, in fact. First, it is safe to say that we should never dabble in something we know nothing about. Hidden dangers lurk around every last corner in this world, and matters of spirituality are no exception. Whether you are a religious person or not, this is a fact, and Sarah learns this in a terrifying and painful way. Unfortunately for her, this lesson comes late.

Secondly, pain is a part of life. All of us go through doubt about our own beliefs and abilities. Sarah's doubt happens to run so deep, and her heart is so broken, that she makes the choice to turn to witchcraft almost strictly out of a sense of revenge toward God. 'If you won't give me my way, I'll find someone who will,' is essentially her thought process. Of course she is hurting, but we all do, and no one is exempt. When we turn our back on our own knowledge and beliefs because we are pouting over the facts of life, we sort of get what we deserve in the end. No amount of revenge or fit throwing will change the fact that bad things happen every single day.

I also try to convey the fact that it is terribly dangerous to give others too much trust. There are those in life that hold positions that should be trustworthy… pastors, parents, teachers, and the like. But we all know too well that everyone is human, and human beings are selfish by nature, not to mention capable of horrible things, no matter what their title or position is. This is especially true if there is something valuable to gain.

First, poor Sarah's grandmother passes while they are together. They are close, and this is the first death the girl ever experiences. She is torn apart, but after a bit, she tries to find her footing in life once again. Right after that, her dog is violently killed; since she is just getting over Grandma, this is like ripping a scab off a wound. Now it is a little harder for her to find her way back into the light. Suddenly, her lifelong best friend is moving two-thousand miles away… another great loss. The final straw is, her mother dies of cancer; all of these things happen in a very short period of time.

Besides her father, the only people she has for support are those from the church, and they are the last people she wants to talk to. Sarah begins to dabble in the craft, just studying and dabbling. After being bullied at school, resulting in personal injury, she decides to cast a spell on the culprit, and much to her great pleasure, it works. Next, she and new boyfriend Ryan Morris cast another, this time for money; this is just to confirm the power at their fingertips.

But things begin to take a scary turn. Ryan gets sick, and Sarah discovers someone evil is controlling the events in Sarah's life from the shadows, and the reason they are doing this is more devious and terrible than anyone can imagine. It takes the help of church member Laura McCain to educate Sarah and help her to confront the darkness which is threatening to consume her.

Yes, once again I have added surprises. Yes, I have twisted things in all the right places. But as I said above, this type of thing would be the nature of the black arts anyway; don't be surprised. The only thing I will admit to here is that I wish things could have gone differently for Sarah in her life; she is a likeable young lady who has promise. Unfortunately, her anger and decisions are her own worst enemy, and ultimately and sadly, this plays out in her life for you to read.

I hope you enjoy reading 'Lucifer's Angel', both for the joy of reading and for the points I have tried to make. It is a creative effort that consists of grief, horror, a bit of romance, and desperation. I have written about witchcraft before, but this story should drive things home and make them a bit more real.

STOLEN BLOOD

ISBN-10: 0997876743 ISBN-13: 978-0997876741

Vampire Thriller

'Stolen Blood' is the story of a secret society of vampires, all of whom live and work among us amicably, without murder or the intent to commit it. The difference between 'Stolen Blood' and other 'functional' vampire works which I have written is that these vampires are able to live the way they do through a pact with the 'Dark Father', to whom they offer a regular sacrifice in return for the ability to live off donated blood.

While I created several vampires who actively participate in this tale, the two main bloodsuckers are Mason Stout and Ira Stone. Mason has worked his way up to be the mayor of Philadelphia, Pennsylvania, while Ira Stone is the head of the massive conglomeration Stone and Kimble Pharmaceuticals. Stone also is the head of the secret society, and along with his wise assistant, is the only one permitted to seek out the will of the Dark Father in any given situation.

This society obtains their blood from a middleman by the name of Ross Berry. Berry is a gambling addict, something of a low-life, but he has the connections needed to obtain donated blood from a company called Bio-Donor, which he, in turn, sells at an atrocious price to the Society. But something happens along the line to Ross, disrupting this 'perfect' arrangement, and motivating Mayor Stout to seek out the assistance of another, Ross's friend and sidekick, Mike Biela. This is when the trouble begins.

The blood obtained by Mike is essentially 'bad', having undergone testing and other unknown 'treatment', which consists of genetic mutation. It is intended for the treatment of cancer, but Mike and those in the Society are unaware of this. Now, Mason Stout and those in his society 'sector' have consumed this blood, and it has reverted them back to the murderous state which they originally possessed. In a blood-induced 'high', Stout kills Mike Biela, and has to find the source of blood for himself, which he does, but only after killing a security guard and single father. Now, Stout must face the guard's grief-stricken and enraged daughter Sasha Hunter, who is being protected under the watchful eyes of Ira Stone; the leader knows that Stout must be stopped if the Society is to have any chance for redemption in the eyes of the Dark Father.

The first point I would like to make, which is vital to the story, is that while Mason Stout is the mayor of a major US city, he is also an egotist whose arrogant condition is aggravated by the bad blood. Sure, he is part of the Society, and he is being cared for by the Dark Father regardless of the negative state of his heart, but when his amplified condition puts all at risk, it is nothing to have to rid the earth of him.

Ira Stone is also a vampire, but his heart is in a much healthier state from the beginning. As the leader of the

Society, it is his responsibility to make sure the others are cared for. Mason Stout manages to lose many who reside in his sector, and this fact alone is enough to make him a liability that needs to go. So, why is the help of the lamenting Sasha Hunter enlisted? Because she is obsessed as well as angry and because Ira is not able to do the deed himself; the elimination of Stout must be done by an outsider. Vigilante justice is the perfect solution.

Now, let's talk about the relationship between Ira and Sasha. Ira quickly gains her trust, almost stepping into the shoes of her deceased father immediately. Though she has no idea that the man is a vampire, she recognizes that he has the same intention as she: To rid the world of the murderous beast that killed her dad, though they both want this for differing reasons. Ira and Sasha quickly become fond of each other, and it takes little to no effort for her to trust this strange older man completely.

'Stolen Blood' is something of a far-fetched story that is heavy with originality and creativity. While it is a story about vampires, it is even more so a story about good versus evil, regardless of the fact that Ira Stone is at the helm when it comes to Mason's demise. It is important to understand that the Society, while made up of vampires, has crossed over into a new existence because of the Dark Father, which has pretty much rendered them 'good guys'.

As a heroine, Sasha Hunter is motivated by rage and deep grief. Anyone could have approached her with the killing of Stout and she would have jumped on the chance. To me, though, it was vital that the 'father figure' type do this, and as the compassionate and sensible leader of the Society, Stone was the ideal candidate to approach her, educate her, and train her, even though he had ulterior motives she has no idea about.

When I wrote this novel, I wanted to put a new skew on the whole vampire idea. This is not the first time I have done this, as long-time fans well know. Anyone familiar with my DeSai Trilogy is already aware that I enjoy creating vampires who live and walk among us, and 'Stolen Blood' is another of that sort.

This is a fun novel which definitely has its horrible moments. The concept is off-beat, but most readers enjoy a change as much as I revel in writing about one.

IN THE DEPTHS

(DeSai Trilogy Book 1)
ISBN-10: 0692721932 ISBN-13: 978-0692721933

Supernatural Thriller

This was the first installment of a vampire trilogy that I wrote involving a witch who is seeking immortality and all power by seducing the omnipotent head vampire of all time. It was also the first vampire book I wrote, and to be honest, one of the most detailed and fun books I have written. I believe that this ongoing saga is deep, engaging, and entertaining.

Cyril DeSai is a centuries-old vampire who has been wreaking havoc and causing terror in the hearts of men the world over. There is more to his behavior than simply murderous feeding; Cyril wants a family of his own that he can lord over and 'love'. In order for that to properly happen, he needs a queen, and finding the right woman is at the heart of his quest. Unfortunately, not just anyone will do; most women give in to his every desire, and he needs one who is capable of taking care of the 'family' in his unforeseen absence, one who will keep his dream alive.

'In the Depths' is written in a manner which allows the fictional vampire characters to live and walk among us. Once DeSai gets the ball rolling by attacking a SCUBA diver in the depths of a cave in Honduras, it is just a matter of time before his kind slowly begins to take over, and this will bring him to full power, in accordance with his plan. The Earth, ultimately, will belong to him, and it will exist only under his rule or the rule of his queen, once she is found. I enjoyed toying with this idea; the thought of all of us wandering around, living our day to day lives without suspicion is basically what we all do every day. Having vampires run the show is pretty much representative of the governments that rule over us. This is one thing that differs in this vampire story when it is compared to others.

Another point that differs and takes this story on its own unique path is the concept of a witch 'mating' with a vampire, and even being bitten for the sole purpose of enjoying life eternal. She is already evil to the core, with her own selfish motives lying at the root of every decision she makes. The outcome, while initially unknown, is the basis for the other two installments in this trilogy, and there are some interesting ideas I added here and there in regards to what would happen if such a union were to take place, even in the fictional realm.

So, with Cyril DeSai seeking all power, Rasia Engres enters the picture. Rasia comes from a long line of witches, and while most of them were 'good' witches (or at least, behaved in a socially acceptable manner), Rasia is rotten through and through. She has basically hated men and their incessant sexual advances for her entire life, so seeking out a true vampire and usurping his plans means nothing to her.

Rasia is strikingly beautiful, with long, lush red hair and emerald eyes. She is slender and toned, and extremely confident in all of her ways. Now, DeSai has always been able to have any woman he wants; he is extremely attractive himself, and his hypnotic manner and ability turn each of them into putty in his hands. Typically, he tires of them quickly, but Rasia is a different story. The beautiful journalist sweeps him off his feet with little effort, and it doesn't take long for the bird to become the prey.

While DeSai is nothing more than a black-hearted spawn of Satan, I wanted him to be somewhat likeable for the reader. I wanted him to be loaded with such sex appeal and confidence that even his most morbid behaviors became easy to overlook. In the first pages, this was a bit difficult, because realistically, Cyril DeSai is a murderous vampire. But once Rasia comes onto the scene, this daunting task lightened a bit. The 'victor' is to become the victim; now the reader is able to sympathize with him on a different level, which honestly sets the tone for both of the next two books.

Is this trilogy far-fetched? Of course! It's a vampire witch story! But it is highly enjoyable directly due to its unbelievability. The point here is not 'Could this really happen'. The point is: what would happen if a witch was able to secure a vampire bite successfully? And what if she was a bad witch by nature? And worse yet, what if she became the head of the most powerful country in the world?

It is also important to point out that, while the people of Earth are all being changed into vampires, those who haven't yet been changed have no idea about the monsters they are surrounded by, and this is part of the big plan. It is an easy takeover for DeSai, a takeover which is based almost slowly on his ability to sweet talk, manipulate and lie. So, is his destiny with Rasia deserved? Almost absolutely! Even after readers learn who he was in the past, before his 'fall' to evil, after they learn of his children and wife, and the way he became who he is, it is impossible to ignore the fact that he is now, a killer. Sympathy may go out the window, but I intended to recreate any feelings of pity one may have for DeSai when I wrote the two follow-up books; I believe I accomplished that goal, as readers will discover when they continue with two and three.

I was highly entertained with the smug, selfish nature of the characters, and it was a joy to bring them to life as I did. I only hope readers enjoy them as much as I did writing them.

WITCHES IMMORTAL

(DeSai Trilogy Book 2)
ISBN-10: 0692722165 ISBN-13: 978-0692722169

Supernatural Thriller

'Witches Immortal' is the second installment in my DeSai Trilogy. Essentially, this series is a vampire tale, but in this, book two, the main character, Rasia Engres, is also a witch. The entire point, besides being an entertaining work of fiction, is to find out about the woman who killed DeSai in book one on a much more personal level.

Rasia is a witch through and through, and she really doesn't have an ounce of love in her soul. This is something I wanted to make clear in 'In the Depths', but even more so here. The most effective way to do that, in my opinion, was to let the readers really get to know her and have an understanding of the reality that a number of circumstances made her who she is. Excuses aside, the woman is evil to the core, and she is truly the perfect mother for the child she is carrying.

So, as readers get to know Rasia, they will also get the scoop on Cyril DeSai from a differing perspective of that given in the first book. Now things are all about the woman who took his life: how she came to know who and what he was, and how she pretty much put herself in a position to take things over. She is crafty and conniving, and she won't think twice about causing pain to another for whatever reason.

Rasia Engres is also a very beautiful woman; her high intelligence level is simply the icing on the cake. She is a tall, slender woman with red hair and green eyes, and her taste in clothing is impeccable. Being a professional woman who is actively climbing the ladder of success, she is able to impose her stern personality often, especially with co-workers and underlings.

Intimate relationships don't really interest her; in fact, she was a virgin when she gave herself to DeSai. Rasia has other things on her mind in life, and they have nothing to do with lying around and making love. She has also been put in very uncomfortable positions by men in her life, as you will read, and this had stirred up a fair amount of rage toward the opposite sex. This point contributes greatly to her virginity being intact for so long in her life.

Rasia can be driven to do 'good', if I could call it that, but only if there is something in it for her. Take, for instance, the serial murderer who is stalking the women of Kiev. Rasia, being a top journalist for the Kiev Post, decides to pursue the killer on her own, and reap the benefits of his sacrifice. For one thing, she is disgusted with what he is doing to women, and she believes he needs to die. But on the other hand, she'll get off killing the murderer anyway, so it's a no-brainer for her to chase him down. Her entire way of thinking is skewed, and any good she does is just the inevitable part of a sick ripple effect.

Now, back to the 'witch' aspect of things. Rasia is not just a witch by practice alone, she is a witch by blood. The line goes back for generations, and let me tell you, these are some husband-killing, child-sacrificing witches. She has been taught by the writings of her Grandmother Anfisa in the sacred Book that if a witch were to sustain a vampire bite, she would not only live eternally, but she would have power unsurpassed, as well. This is the driving force behind everything Rasia Engres does in her life, from her career choice to every last sacrifice; if there is a true vampire walking the earth, Rasia intends to find him.

Once she finds him, however, he must bite her, and she is pretty sure that it isn't easy to dictate who a vampire will bite. The good news is she is stunningly beautiful, she is accomplished, and as a witch, she is somewhat resistant to DeSai's more hypnotic qualities. Rasia is a confident woman with a strong mindset: Come hell or high water, she will get her bite.

She doesn't sound like someone who would have enough nurturing ability in her little finger to birth and raise a child, but by the end of the book, it is obvious that is exactly what she is going to do. It is here that I realized it was important to soften her up a bit, no matter how little. Yes, she is going to have a baby, but she is still a terrible person; I felt the best approach was for her to begin to rue the killing of Cyril, and maybe she realizes that she loved him just a bit. This is a burden that Rasia Engres must bear for her own eternity.

'In the Depths' and 'Witches Immortal' are basically the story of a vampire and a witch who make a baby; the trilogy will culminate with his birth and life in book three. Cyril DeSai was a manipulative vampire who actually began to take over the world. Rasia Engres is the beautiful witch who rips it all from his hands. Their child will put them both to shame. When discussing only Rasia, however, she can stand on her own two feet in any situation, with no exception. While I despised her as a person, I loved her as a character, and she was actually one of my favorites to write about. She will continue on in book three, and fans will get to see how life, and its random series of events, brings everyone to their knees, including vampires and witches.

I had fun writing 'Witches Immortal', and I hope you get just as much enjoyment out of it when you read it. I found it entertaining to develop the character of Rasia, taking over with her from 'In the Depths', and I don't believe you will be disappointed. The woman certainly is evil through and through.

LUCIEN'S REIGN

(DeSai Trilogy Book 3)
ISBN-10: 069272219X ISBN-13: 978-0692722190

Supernatural Thriller

The third and final book in my DeSai Trilogy is entitled 'Lucien's Reign', and it tells the story of the culmination of Cyril DeSai and Rasia Engres in their son, Lucien. Ultimately, Lucien's existence has been the key all along; his mother Rasia and even his father Cyril were only mere pawns in the game the Powers are playing. This final installment chronicles his life until he finally comes into complete power at the age of eighteen.

At the very beginning of the book, Rasia is in the throes of labor. Now, to readers who are familiar with her character from reading the first two, she is a hard, dark woman with nothing but evil intent in her heart. She has murdered the vampire Cyril DeSai, but not until after they have made passionate love. Pregnant with his child, she picked up his mantle and continued on as his wife and head of the new DeSai family, which he has been creating.

Rasia is aware that her son is something of a 'chosen' one. He has a purpose set firmly in stone by the Powers, and the fact that he is the most horrific of breeds, a cross between a vampire and a witch, makes him dangerous from the beginning. At times, you may notice that she is apprehensive when it comes to him, almost as if she is afraid of him. Because she is so hateful, it is a bit satisfying, in a sense, for her to be fearful of another, particularly her own child.

Her trepidation turns out to be justified: Lucien is the son of Satan himself; not a man, but an animal with insatiable appetites that he cannot even begin to comprehend. So basic are these instincts, and so powerful, that Lucien doesn't even give them a second's consideration. He simply does what feels good and what pleases him at the moment.

The birth of Lucien Cerebus DeSai is nothing but a threat to Rasia, and this interferes with her affection. She is afraid of the Powers, as she should be, so she confirms. Otherwise, as far as her son goes, he is nothing more than the one who would take the rule from her hands; she would eventually be his slave. She hates him, deep inside; there is really not an ounce of true affection in her soul for the boy she carries and births.

I wanted a certain level of normalcy and balance to remain in the world in this book, even though the majority of the population are vampires. The only way to accomplish this was through the mean-spirited Rasia; I had to play up her mothering instincts, and I had to make Cyril's family dream become her dream as well. Only in this way would she raise Lucien with the iron fist necessary for him to become an effective family head. All character defects aside, she does the best she can; she schools him herself and basically keeps him isolated, with the exception of a single female friend, who eventually becomes his betrothed.

Isabella Scarlet Gilliam is the daughter of Patrick, the first bitten by DeSai while on a scuba diving trip when DeSai began to build his family. She is the voice of reason and the rock of stability throughout Lucien's life; she knows him like no other, bearing witness to, and keeping all of his secrets. She adores him as the night adores the moon, and she looks forward to the day she will be his wife. She, like Lucien, is a 'half-breed'. Her mother is human a majority of Isabella's life. Lucien is unaware of his witch vampire lineage until later in the book, as you will see.

Isabella also suffers an abundance of heartache and grief when it comes to her love. At one point, Lucien goes through a sort of 'vampire puberty' that sends him off on insane sexual tangents. For a long period, he completely puts Isabella out of his life, and she attempts to go on with her own, her love continuing to burn. But her own mother Rose will not allow her to have a relationship with another because Isabella's marriage to Lucien is inevitable; it is the will of the Powers. The girl must bear her burdens alone.

I should also mention the other signs of wickedness that Lucien displays in his life, though more often than not, are only visible to you, the reader. Rasia knows he is sick, but she is unaware of all he really does; he is deceitful and conniving like no other child before him, and he hides his fun and games well. Rasia finds herself on her knees before the powers, even asking to end her own son's life, to no avail. The Powers demand that she fulfill her given task: To raise the boy to maturity and power.

Writing 'Lucien's Reign' was a good time; I was able to really cut loose in a lot of areas regarding the true enormity of Lucien's evil character while attempting to help readers embrace any iota of humanity that he may possess. I believe I also dealt justice wisely to Rasia for all of her sins, and I think that the reader will agree. For those who have read this book, or the entire series, I do hope you had as much fun with these sick characters as I have.

ABOUT THE AUTHOR

I am a father of two beautiful children, Jon and Kim. They are my motivating forces; they are the lighthouse in this vast ocean. In this life, they are the air that I breathe; they are the oasis in this desert of uncertainty. They are my greatest joy in life, and my number one priority. I have a long list of hobbies, and I attribute that to my lust for life! I like to surround myself with positive people, who share the same interests. Family values, the arts, outdoors, nature, and travel are tops on my list. I embrace attending cultural and artistic events because I believe dramatic self-expression is the window to the soul. I wear my heart on my sleeve, and I still believe in chivalry, and I always treat people the way I want to be treated.

www.rwkclark.com

85845521R00188

Made in the USA
Lexington, KY
05 April 2018